TARGET FREEDOM TOWER

TOWER

Terror At The Rising

by

Thomas A. Vinton

INTRODUCTION

Following a career in the FBI and a stint as the Deputy Commissioner of the Westchester County Police, I had the opportunity to work as an integrity monitor at Tower 1, commonly known as The Freedom Tower. It was the rebuilding of the World Trade Center destroyed by terrorists on 9/11. I checked for no-show jobs, the security of equipment, correct delivery invoices and prepared daily reports. A welcome change from the stodgy suit and tie of my past was the hard hat, reflective vest and construction boots.

For seven years I had the opportunity to observe and interact with some of the most patriotic, hardworking men and women representing the various trades that engulfed the site. Resentful at first, they gradually loosened up, accepted my presence, and eventually treated me as one of them, not as a "suit" meddling in their work. I made new friends.

This, with my law enforcement experience and

a vivid imagination, gave me the idea for this novel. I believe it is something that could have happened without the vigilance of the monitors, but primarily the vigilance of the many workers there who never want to see another 9/11.

Some of the characters from my previous novel *The Package* return, in particular Dick Gerosa who mirrors my good friend Dick Genova, a talented and dedicated undercover agent who departed this life all too soon.

The photo on the cover was taken by Eva Klanduchova whose work can be found at Pexels.com.

CHAPTER 1

Freedom Tower construction site, New York City

Not if but when.

Fifty stories up, Eddie Michaels gazed over the two-by-four railing that separated him from the ground. Below, people were coming, going and some just milling about admiring the project. They were mere specs on the concrete below.

Will always be a target but hopefully I'll be gone before then.

"Coming through." Two laborers carrying rebar interrupted his thoughts as they began to edge past him. He pressed himself against the outer railing of the four foot wide catwalk that hugged the perimeter, and hoped that the carpenters did a good job nailing it together.

"Thank you, boss," one of them said, knowing by his age, soft hands, and smooth complexion that he was someone more important than them. The clanging of carpenters' hammers as they installed steel concrete forms in preparation for the pouring of high-density concrete rang in his ears, but he was used to it. This was big league construction, and it was winter.

Hooded sweatshirts worn beneath hard hats, and heavy Carhartt coats, gloves and ear protectors kept the cutting Hudson River wind from burning their extremities. In the summer, tee shirts of all shapes and imprints and makeshift shrouds protecting the back of their necks from the sun were standard garb.

Reflective vests were mandatory, the griminess of which were badges of tenure. Along with eye protection, they were targets of the safety inspectors who roamed the site looking for violations, resulting in heavy fines or firings. Smoking was the worst.

"We're moving up. Hopefully a floor every ten days if the ironworkers and concrete workers can get their act together," said the harried superintendent of the construction management company as he stopped next to Michaels. A two-way radio clipped to his blue jeans, a button-down shirt under his vest and untied construction boots differentiated him from the others.

"When are the numbers going to increase?" asked Michaels, not only to make conversation but in connection with his work there.

"They'll be like cockroaches in the next few months. Electricians, plumbers, HVAC workers and drywall carpenters have skeleton crews, but they will soon increase. It's growing exponentially as the floors go up. Gonna make my job more of a pain in the ass. This will probably be my swan song." Mike Spinelli was referring to the flood of additional tradesmen that would arrive as the structure ascended during the next three years.

"Doubt it Mike," Michaels said. "It's in your blood. Besides, you like the interviews on the channel 2 Evening News."

Spinelli disregarded the remark because he knew it was true. "You know, Eddie, many of the ironworkers here did the deconstruction of the World Trade Center towers when they were brought down on 9/11 and have strong feelings."

"I know that," said Michaels. He was referring to the imprints on tee shirts, sweatshirts, and hard hats. "I didn't forget – I don't forgive" under a small flag, was popular. Veterans wore miniatures of their military seal on their hardhats along with several other stickers; some representing their local union and some American flags with various sayings.

"You know the crawler crane down below," said Spinelli. "The operator has an American and a United States Marine Corps flag mounted on the rear of his cab. He was wounded in Vietnam, and the sophisticated machine he's operating is critical to the safe construction of this building. They're all patriots, proud to be working here and not ashamed to display it."

"I still worry." Michaels responded as he glanced at the tower crane rising from the core of the structure. He looked at his watch and saw that he had another hour before he could get the hell out of there.

"No matter how safe everything appears, I still worry about the tower and the thousands of commuters that use the PATH trains and come and go daily through the makeshift entrance next to us. We've all heard it before. We have to be right all of the time, while they only have to be right once."

"I have confidence in you guys." The super turned from Michaels and looked into the core where several workers were assembled. "And see those guys in there. Whether you like unions or not, there are all solid hard-working Americans and are proud of their work. To them and future workers, it will always be The Freedom Tower and not Tower 1. You and I know the reason why they changed it: Tower 1 is an easier name to sell to lessees."

Spinelli leaned on the railing looking down with Michaels. "Eddie, I'm not prying, but what the hell do you do here and why you?

"I'll give you the Reader's Digest version." The seasoned FBI agent didn't want to admit this was not a choice assignment, but he had to bitch to someone other than his girlfriend.

"Did you ever hear of Pappy Mason, the largest

heroin dealer in New York?" Michaels turned towards Spinelli.

"Yeah, I read about it in the papers."

"I was in charge of the Drug Enforcement Task Force that took him down. It was my informant that made the case, and I was a rock star. The downside is that informants are treacherous and when the DEA knew he was working for us, they took him down. Rather than go to jail, he turned on me and said I was taking money and everything else. That shit really excites another federal agency, and it makes headlines. Fortunately, he eventually did the right thing and told the truth, but the damage had been done with the newspapers playing it up and getting daily leaks." Michaels paused. "You could eventually find my exoneration on page 20."

"I don't get it. So how did you end up down here?"

"My career was shot. They took me off of drug enforcement, busted me down to a street agent and assigned me to the Joint Terrorism Task Force referred to as the JTTF. I've got a year to retire and got assigned here because I was the new guy and everyone else wanted to dig up terrorist cells here in New York. Frankly, it sucks. I'm used to being active, and now I'm counting the hours before I can get out of here."

Spinelli shook his head. "Sounds like something my company would do. Super Structure is all over the world and has thousands of employees, but this job is their showcase. If someone from the company or anyone on the site screws up, it lands on me, and I go back as a super on a doghouse. If things go well, I'm a hero. The Port Authority looks good, and everyone drinks champagne, and I move on to another big job."

They turned to the dots below until Spinelli broke the silence.

"So, what's your job here? I get asked that several times a day. That is, if you can talk about it. They know you are FBI and speculate on all kinds of secret missions."

Michaels grinned. "Nothing as James Bondish as you might think. When they needed a body to monitor the construction here, a job active agents would try to avoid, being a new guy on the JTTF, I was it. My job – hang around, speak to workers, to see if anyone was being influenced by Islamic jihadists or any other terrorists who would like to see it go down before completion, mirroring the 9/11 terrorist strike. There are splinter groups out there, and they wanted to break the spirit of New Yorkers who rallied around Giuliani and came together with an 'in your face' attitude and showed the world how resilient they were.

"Specifically, I check the security of the architects' drawings, spot check the backgrounds done by the security company screening all the workers, look for no show jobs and the possible influence of organized crime on the local unions who have people here. Very fucking exciting." His sarcasm was evident.

Spinelli shook his head again. "If you're focusing on the Middle East people working here there's not many of them."

"You got that right, but I'm checking all of them."

"But isn't that profiling?" Spinelli laughed.

"Most certainly is," Michaels said. "But I don't give a shit. What are they going to do to me?"

Spinelli's phone buzzed. "Got to take this," he said as he walked away giving Michaels a wave.

An easy job for some, but Michaels was not made for this. He worked eight to five or whatever hours he wanted to make. Hard hat, construction boots and a reflective vest were now the uniform of the day, a far cry from the customary business suit. No FBI emblazoned on the back like a raid jacket, but almost all the workers there knew who he was. Some avoided him because they were felons who beat the required background check. Some liked to hear Bureau war stories.

He had been there for over a year and knew all of the foremen and superintendents representing the several trades, primarily the concrete workers comprised of lathers, carpenters, and laborers. Michaels moved about the site in an attempt to keep his forty-nine-year-old body in shape. He introduced himself to workers as he went up and down wooden and aluminum ladders inside the core leading to the catwalks. He watched as lathers installed vertical rebar and the carpenters installed forms in preparation for a concrete pour. Fear of heights was not an option. He had to show the workers that he was capable of going wherever they went, or he would be nothing more than a "suit" that would be ridiculed.

Michaels spent much of his idle time thinking about his girlfriend, Nancy Schaeffer. They met two years ago when she was a domestic flight attendant, and he had a first class upgrade returning from an FBI conference in Los Angeles.

"Chateau screw top, I presume, and February of this year was a good month," he said as she poured his first glass of wine when the 747 leveled off.

She leaned closer and whispered, "It's free and so is your upgrade, so please don't insult a nice California Cabernet." The large aircraft hit an air pocket and dropped quickly, forcing Nancy off balance, and thrusting her breasts against Eddie's face. To steady herself, she reached for the tray and tipped over the partially filled glass, spilling wine over the crotch of his gray trousers. Her other hand, holding the bottle, tipped in the same motion, and spilled more of the ruby red on his canary yellow sport coat.

Both were embarrassed at the collision of body parts and the spilled wine.

"That'll take about three quarts of seltzer water to straighten out," she said with a weak smile. "You know the old flight attendant trick to get stains out."

He could only shake his head and grin. He took off his coat and handed it to her. "What about the pants?" he asked with another grin.

"Can't help you in that department," she said. "It would be considered a crime aboard an aircraft for you to sit here with no pants on, and I would have to ask the pilot to radio ahead for the FBI, who would have to arrest you."

Eddie showed her his badge and credentials and they both laughed.

"Listen, I'm based in New York, and I'm done after this flight. If you want, I'll buy you a drink when I get off to make up for this," said Nancy.

"Sounds good, only if I can drive you home. I have my car in the Port Authority Police lot. That is, if you're not married or living with some guy."

"No to both questions."

They began dating and a few months later, when the lease was up on her Manhattan apartment, she moved to within a block of Michaels in the Bronx. Neither saw marriage in the future and they both wanted their space for the time being, so they agreed to the current arrangement rather than living together. For Michaels, Nancy filled a void after his wife left him. Nancy was a good friend and bedmate. He was on a rebound from his marriage, and Nancy wanted steady companionship. Now she wanted more. Marriage was not in his vocabulary but became a regular topic. He had to decide in the near future.

"What now Eddie, what new windmill is Don Quixote going to chase?" she would ask him sarcastically whenever he started a new case on the drug task force. The long hours on surveillance and meeting informants usually followed by a few drinks with his co-workers in a local watering hole always continued. His new assignment seemed to stabilize his hours, and now it was a matter of legitimizing his relationship or moving on. He called it the M word and tried to avoid its discussion. He cut back on his drinking and was back to going to the health club in an effort to turn back the clock on his aging body.

Back at street level, an overweight middle-aged security guard wearing an ill-fitting blue uniform approached Michaels. "Here's the list of the new passes that were issued." Without waiting for a response, the guard meandered back to the security trailer on the site. SECURITY was plastered across the back of his vest.

Michaels scanned the spreadsheet containing a list of those who recently passed the cursory background check done by a security company. He was looking for any unusual names. Later, he would run them through the terrorist database at the office to see if any were relatives or associates of anyone of interest to the JTTF. None of the names on the spreadsheet, including the name

Kieran Burke, at first glance meant anything to him.

That would all change.

CHAPTER 2

A hunting lodge in Wyndham, NY

Federal judge Robert Kirkland lectured as he sat in an overstuffed leather chair in the small two-bedroom stone cabin. He nursed a snifter glass of twelve-year-old scotch as embers from the fireplace radiated warmth.

"See those." Kirkland pointed to a wall covered with memorabilia from conservative religious and civic groups in appreciation for his work on the bench. "I've been around for a while and people appreciate what I have done in my sixty plus years. But there is more to do, and we need a visceral reaction from the President, the Congress and the people, if we are to succeed." His audience of two listened attentively. "Remember, democracy and freedom are not negotiable."

Kirkland digressed as he ran his hand through long gray hair swept back over chiseled features that topped a solid six-foot frame. "I love the courtroom, particularly intimidating the phony counsels that are milking guilty defendants of thousands of dollars, putting on a show when they know the guy is guilty. Years on the bench have given me a low tolerance for these scum, and I enjoy overruling their objections and cautioning them against long-winded opening statements and closing arguments."

The law was his love. He lived alone in a New York City apartment and shunned social events. Trips to the cabin were a brief respite from the stodgy judicial world of legal briefs and court transcripts.

He came from a long line of lawyers, most of whom became partners in some of New York's most prestigious white shoe law firms billing seven hundred plus dollars an hour. But it wasn't the money for Judge Kirkland. It was the power over the destiny of other human beings.

Kirkland took his eyes off the wall and looked at his guests. "I tend to bloviate, please forgive me. But age is catching up, and I like to reminisce. Back to the reason why we are here. Our plan has to be foolproof. There is no margin for error and as we all know, there is a lot at stake for all of us."

Edmund Whitaker, president and CEO of Coordinated Technologies, arrived earlier with Kirkland in a helicopter that landed in a custom clearing in the woods behind the cabin. He was now seated across from Kirkland in a matching couch.

"West Point, a tour in Iraq and six years in the

army taught me to be precise in what I do, and I've maintained and cultivated contacts in the Defense Department, contacts only available to West Point alums that will facilitate what we want to do."

In his early forties, Whitaker sported a crew cut and maintained a disciplined exercise routine evidenced by his military bearing.

Kirkland ignored his remark and got to the point. "Where do we stand?" he asked.

Whitaker thought for a moment. "I now can manufacture a product far superior to what the military has, and should the United States enter into a major conflict, I could gain financially aside from satisfying my personal beliefs. As we discussed, a portion of this would go to enhance your position for whatever you choose, perhaps Attorney General or the Supreme Court." Whitaker paused as Kirkland nodded in agreement.

Whitaker continued. "The obstacle is obviously the president and the war weary people who put him in office. The world's other superpowers are poking him to see how far they can go. Iran and Russia know they are dealing with a novice, and a defiant radical Muslim population is gaining a foothold throughout the world. I agree that it is going to take a catastrophic event to turn this mindset around, and we should move forward quickly."

Coordinated Technologies was a hazy name for a manufacturer and supplier of armament to the military. Whitaker's connections facilitated a no-bid contract with the Defense Department to enhance the effectiveness of drone missiles in order to minimize collateral damage among other armament improvements. Not a defense contractor on official records, he maintained a small office in suburban Rye, New York, ostensibly for the building and integration of sophisticated computer systems. Whitaker amassed considerable wealth that included a house on the grounds of a prestigious country club and the luxury of a late model Cadillac Escalade for him and a Mercedes S550 for his wife, Christine. His daughter Debbie attended a top Ivy League school.

Whitaker and Kirkland belonged to Westchester Hall Country Club where their similar conservative political views drew them together. More importantly, they had the wherewithal and will to do something about their distaste for the direction the country was going in. They shared these on the golf course, or in the club bar, but never in the presence of other members.

Their attention was now on Michael Zorn, who had just arrived in his Range Rover, which navigated a half mile of rocky road from the Interstate, left unrepaired to discourage hunters from going near the cabin. He was presently the New York State Homeland Security adviser for a salary of a dollar a year.

"Just to update you, my CIA background

and my new position gives me access to weekly security briefings held by a representative of National Homeland Security at the New York Office of the FBI. More important, it gives me access to the files of several state and local government agencies."

The youngest of the three, he was a contrast to the others. Blue jeans, unkempt hair and slightly overweight were a cover for a sharp analytical mind. He was there because Kirkland knew Zorn's father, a wealthy philanthropist who donated freely to conservative causes and who was instrumental in getting Kirkland appointed to his judgeship. Kirkland became a surrogate father to young Michael following his father's premature death and steered him through Princeton and then into the CIA, where he saw that Michael received assignments that would give him experience and future contacts. Money was no object as he was an only child and received a substantial inheritance upon his father's death.

Unbeknownst to Zorn at the time, Kirkland had plans for him. They evolved two years earlier. He had ten years in the agency, service in five foreign stations, and with Kirkland's influence, developed distaste for the way that the present administration tied the hands of the CIA and was making them scapegoats in circus like trials where they had to defend previously accepted routine actions. He left the CIA, and at Kirkland's urging, took the Homeland Security position where he believed that he could be instrumental in bringing about Kirkland and Whittaker's dream of having the United States regain its position as the world's foremost superpower.

This could only be done by a massive commitment of the military in preemptive strikes to destroy all those who, in the opinion of the three, wanted to destroy America. Zorn had the catalyst to make this happen, the reward for him being monetary and political power. The three were alone and could talk openly in the security of the cabin.

Zorn began his presentation as he always did at the bi-weekly meetings of the group.

"They are about three months behind schedule because of the normal bickering between the ironworkers and the concrete contractor. But that is normal. It should proceed close to schedule. Inspectors are all over the place ensuring compliance with the specs, and sometimes they slow things down when the concrete has to be chipped away and other adjustments made to the original building plans."

Whitaker stopped him. "I realize that you have no control over the time frame, but we can't wait until 105 floors are up, or even seventy five. It will then be too late. I have a lot of money ready to be invested, but my investors want to see some kind of return. It is private money, not institutional, so we can control it somewhat. But investors get impatient. As you know, I lost a lot of Afghanistan money because my lobbyists didn't grease the right politicians. I do not intend for that to happen this time."

Kirkland interjected. "I want to reiterate that this is also a moral issue. I've spent an inordinate amount of time speaking to deaf ears as to what our world position should be, but with this new administration everyone wants to play peacemaker and apologist. Meanwhile, the terrorists are laughing at us. They see us a paper tiger. I've spoken with many of my associates and have lobbied strongly to keep terrorists from receiving a Miranda warning instead of being treated like enemy combatants. It was only a stroke of luck that we were able to keep Gitmo open and keep legal proceedings out of New York. You can't do that with these people."

Kirkland took a sip of his scotch, leaned forward in his chair, and glanced at the other two. "I've never been more serious. A preemptive strike is the only way for us to handle this. By us, I mean our country. And believe me, there are many with whom I have been in contact who would support such an action. They only need a reason, and hopefully we can supply them with one. How are we doing with our direct site intelligence? Did we get anyone in there yet?"

"I think I got a good break after checking out all the people down there for the last two months. As you know, I can get the background check reports prepared by the security company because of my position with Homeland Security" Zorn answered. "They are limited in what they do and mainly just check for local felony arrests. I dig deeper and run their names through the CIA indices. I came up with something interesting.

"There is an Irishman who just came into the country and who was able to hook up with Local 18A, the Irish laborers local working there.

"A little strange for him to get work right away when there are plenty of people out of work. Are you sure he is with us?" Kirkland was thinking like a judge, thought Zorn.

"Ironically, he fit right in. Checking on him through the CIA, he came from County Kerry, where most of the 18A laborers come from, and like many of the Irish, hates the English even though there is a peace. In Ireland, our guy wanted to rejuvenate the IRA and start the bombings again. Didn't know what the hell he was talking about politically, but wore the Irish hate for the English on his sleeve. The business manager of Local 18A got his name, probably from a relative, and called his contacts in Kerry to learn about him. Not necessarily his political beliefs, but to see if he was a worker and to make sure he would do nothing to embarrass the local. Someone put in the good word for him."

"How does that make him fit into our plan?" asked Kirkland, again being skeptical.

Zorn smiled. "The files I checked showed that

after his most anti-English IRA associates rejected most of his ideas, he went to England and took up with Muslim extremists who are always trying to stir up trouble with the English."

Kirkland leaned forward in his chair, interested.

How do we know this?"

"He was monitored by MI-5," said Zorn, "who passed the info to the CIA when our guy came to the states three months ago. He didn't seem important enough to be closely scrutinized, but I saw the info, so I volunteered to keep an eye on him under the guise of turning him for intelligence purposes."

"What about the CIA?"

"My former associates didn't care what I did with him and, being shorthanded, they gave me the green light to do what I want. I now have a cover if I am picked up on surveillance."

"Where are we going with this?" Kirkland again interrupted. "Am I missing something?"

"Judge, bear with me on this. I can mold this guy to do probably anything that I want him to do. I had one of our people do an informal psychological profile on him, and he basically is a good candidate for suggestive behavior. He takes suggestions easily, particularly when they fit in with his beliefs. I believe that we can not only use him for information, but he could be our prime mover down the line."

"Sounds like the Manchurian Candidate

revisited," said Whitaker, captured by the idea of suggestive behavior.

Zorn continued, "You are partially correct. When Richard Condon wrote, he had no idea that he was providing fuel for thought for the CIA. A well-kept secret is that the CIA still has a branch that specializes in controlling the behavior of others to unwittingly do their bidding. Many times, this can be accomplished simply by repetitive suggestions to the vulnerable subject combined with a form of hypnosis. There are rumors that behavior can be affected by radio wave impulses from a short distance and, although the Agency tried that in the '60s, nothing definite came from it except fuel for the conspiracy theorists. Sometimes drugs, similar to LSD, are used to enhance and speed up the suggestive behavior and that has been proven. I have access to these drugs and the experts to instruct me how to use them. I cannot go into any detail – it is beyond top secret and my full knowledge is limited. Suffice to say that it would be disavowed by anyone in government, and anyone suggesting that it exists would be characterized as delusional."

"All of this sounds a little confusing and somewhat futuristic or out of a spy novel, but keep going. I'm willing to at least listen." Kirkland sat back, looking at Zorn.

"I'm not going to be talking directly to our Irish friend in my official capacity." continued Zorn, "That would make no sense. I have an intermediary, and it will all come together."

Kirkland rose and paced about, head down, rubbing his chin with his right hand. Whitaker and Zorn waited in silence.

"Always was deliberate in making my decisions from the bench. Always considered how I could impact society and further my personal beliefs, not necessarily interpreting the law. Never would have made it to the Supreme Court." He smiled briefly. "Let us assume what you say is true. Seeing that you don't intend to have direct contact with the man, how is this going to happen?"

Zorn was delighted in how he could keep the questions coming, the answers to which he already had. It was a game he played with the two successful men he was with, whose intelligence surpassed his.

"I have an operative who can get close to him, in fact so close she will sleep with him. She was a paid CIA asset who was given sanctuary in the U. S. a few years back, so I scooped her up and put her on the payroll. I was her handler. Doesn't care what she has to do, doesn't ask questions, and is happy as long as she gets her paycheck, which I might add, is substantial. The CIA dropped her at my request right before I left because she was no longer productive. I kept her on the hook in case I could use her for something in the future outside the boundaries of the Agency.

"She is perfect for this assignment, and I have

continued her payments out of our slush fund. She still thinks she is working for the CIA, who was gracious enough to let me continue to use my covert meeting spot and contact number because of the security clearance with my Homeland Security position. They think I am wasting my time with her and believe I only contact her every few months to see what, if anything, she has. She has done some good work for us in the past, no questions asked."

"How secure is she for what we want?" Kirkland stopped his pacing and stood in front of Zorn.

"When all this is over, she can be put out to pasture somewhere in the west with a steady income, which we can pay for, or I'll see she gets it from the CIA because I will fabricate a story that her life is in danger. They have deep pockets and something like this would be easy. She'll keep her mouth shut, not that anyone would believe her anyway. And if she doesn't, I can handle it"

"Sounds like something out of the movies," Whitaker remarked. "How does all this tie together?"

"I've had her schooled in the process of suggestive behavior, and in a relatively short time she will have the Irishman ready to do what she wants. If not, there are the drugs. Meanwhile, I pull the strings like a puppet master, and she gets all the intelligence that we need. Particularly about the core structure, amount of concrete and rebar and what it would take to bring a portion of it down. More important, the work schedule and who will be there and on what days.

"We want to limit the loss of life, but I do not believe that is possible. Right now, from what I hear, there are about 700 workers of the various trades at the site. As it goes up, this will increase rapidly until there are over 2,000. If we wait until then, our task will be much more difficult. Not only will we be unable to substantially damage the structure, but there will be considerable loss of life. Although loss of life is not palatable, I'm sure we all agree that it might be necessary to generate the response that we want. It has to have Al-Qaeda written all over it, directed from Afghanistan with a follow up threat by Iran, who has duped us for years about a nuclear bomb. Is this Bush and Iraq again?"

"That's a good question," remarked Kirkland. "That was a perfect storm but was mishandled by Bush's advisors. A shame. With a little chicanery by the right people, we could have rolled across almost all of the Mideast and be knocking at the door of Russia and China. Saudi Arabia, Kuwait, Iran, Pakistan and all those other Muslim countries would all be ours along with all of their oil."

"This time it will be different," Zorn said. "There will be more paper to back it up. From my briefings, I see that more and more information is coming in from overseas that Iran is preparing to take out Israel with provisions to stop the US from interfering by neutralizing us through a preemptive strike. Al-Qaeda is getting stronger since we left a void in Iraq when our troops left. And I am hearing about a terrorist group called ISIS, the Islamic State of Iran and Syria that is in its embryonic stage but makes Al-Qaeda look like boy scouts. The information is foggy but somewhat credible; credible enough to set in motion our warmonger politicians." Zorn paused.

"What else?" asked Whitaker.

"We are getting ready to pull out of Afghanistan, and it appears that Karzai is cutting a deal with the Taliban. Al-Qaeda is flocking there as a training base. Intelligence is coming in every day about this, so what would be a logical target?"

Another pause as Zorn gave Kirkland and Whitaker time to digest what he said up to this point. "You have to understand, our man has marginal intelligence, otherwise none of this would work. And in the end, he is no longer here and really no one will care."

Kirkland resumed pacing. "I want to correct your earlier statement. Loss of life is palatable. As distasteful as it is, it is necessary for the reaction we want. But when all this is over, what will the press and all of our premier investigative agencies say? One crazy Irishman and not even a member of Al-Qaeda. A lone wolf incident of terrorism. How will this generate the anger that came after 9/11, enough anger to launch an attack against whomever the powers decide? Enough to level Afghanistan or join with Israel in neutralizing Iran, or if we are lucky, the North Koreans decide to jump in, and we level their country with a couple of nuclear bombs. All that would put us back to the power in the world that we used to enjoy, but we need the initial rush to judgment. That's what we need, but one crazy Irishman will not do it."

"Good question." said Zorn, "Right now I am starting to build a local CIA file regarding him. As you know, I have access to their files because of my present position and my background. They have the original info about him being followed by M I-5 because of his terrorist sympathies. I've added several pieces of information to the file from the station chief in London, who recently had a fatal heart attack. I backdated the email reports and put the supervisor's initials on them, which he will deny when they surface, but no one will believe him. They will need a scapegoat. I also covertly added a lot of contemporary false documentation from assets operating in London and the Mideast who reported on the Irishman, saying how he secretly communicated with Al-Qaeda elements in London who were going to fund his entrance into the United States with the goal of committing an act of terrorism that would gain national attention. I didn't mention where he is working, but when it all falls out, and the dots are connected, it will be obvious what the target was. What better way to come under the radar of the

FBI than to have an Irishman do the dirty work of Al-Qaeda.

"Interesting, but what is the time frame?"

"Judge, to get enough collateral damage it has to be done when a large number of workers are involved. They are now working weekends, and more are coming on for day work. Enough collateral damage will happen. I'd say two months. Possibly on 9/11, or a day or two after to make the connection."

"Are you secure in what you are doing? What if someone finds out about your visits up here? We have reason but you don't," the judge said.

"We are all here for the same reason. Relax for a weekend, play cards, and have a few drinks. That's what the pilot who shuttles you back and forth believes. Nothing more. It is common knowledge that you are my surrogate father who guided me through my younger days and now still gives me career advice. There is nothing out of the ordinary with me meeting you up here every couple of weeks. Also, I drive while you take the chopper. And my wife thinks I'm on some secret Agency business that I can't tell her about."

Small talk continued as Kirkland put some aged strip steaks on the indoor grill and selected a good bottle of Cabernet from a closet that he had made into a mini wine cellar. After eating, Zorn exchanged pleasantries with Kirkland and Whitaker and departed back to Westchester in his SUV.

Kirkland poured two snifter glasses with Hennessy brandy, gave one to Whitaker, and returned to his chair.

"How confident are you in this kid?" asked Whitaker.

"I brought him along to this point. He's smart, knows the system, and is in a perfect position. However, if this whole thing ever gets too close to us, I will leave it up to you to make him disappear. It would hurt me, but we agree that the end justifies the means whatever it takes. Do you agree and are you capable of handling that if necessary?"

Whitaker nodded.

Kirkland mused, "It's a disgrace how the bureaucrats at the Port Authority changed the name Freedom Tower to Tower One because the designation would discourage tenants for fear of being a target. Next to the footprint of the former World Trade Center it is almost unpatriotic. Hopefully, all the controversy from its inception will be a moot point and the pompous federal and local law enforcement officials who pride themselves of providing the utmost in impenetrable security will be left with egg on their face. A good lesson for arrogance."

CHAPTER 3

Katonah Avenue, Bronx, NY

Katonah Avenue, in the northern section of the Bronx, is the home to Irish émigrés and has the distinct reputation of having the most bars of any street in New York City.

"This one's on me," is a common phrase by bartenders putting an inverted shot glass on the bar in front of a customer, hoping his pub and his dream would not come and go like many of the others who couldn't make it.

"How was it down there, today?" they would ask a sandhog who dug the tunnels beneath the city or, "You still bustin' your ass as a lugger?" or "Did they make you a flagman finally?" they would ask a laborer who carried rebar.

Similar questions appropriate to the trade would be asked the floor finishers, union reps and truck drivers. The bartenders knew by name all the blue-collar workers who prided themselves on their strong backs.

"And what will be your pleasure today, Rosie – Bridie - Maeve," or whoever. They were always polite to the waitresses, domestics and hotel workers, who were the counterparts of the blue-collar men, and knew if they were there, the men would follow.

Thursday night to Sunday afternoon, male and female come together in their favorite watering holes where "Make it a Guinness" or just "Jamison" echoed while hard earned money is dropped on the worn oak bars and jokes and stories of the old country are traded.

She was neither red haired nor freckled nor had the fair Irish skin, but could easily pass for one of the descendants of the Spanish Armada's unintended landing on the coast of Ireland. Dressed in a pair of casual blue slacks and a full cut light gray sweater that left her shape up to the imagination, she deliberately made her way to a spot behind the thin construction worker as Irish music blasted in the Piper's Lounge on this particular evening. Some of the single bar crowd eyed her as she passed them, while others were openly aggressive in their remarks fueled by their alcoholic intake. Besides the music, three televisions over the bar had a replay of one of the soccer games involving Ireland's national team, which brought periodic roars from the patrons.

The man whose picture and background she had studied for days was now in front of her.

"Fer Christ's sake," he said when his pint of

Guinness partially spilled on the bar. He spun around expecting one of the regulars, but stopped mid-sentence when he saw her.

It was 8:00 pm and he had been there since his workday ended. His dirty blue jeans and steel toed boots were unchanged and labeled him as a laborer. A plaid cotton shirt covered a black tee shirt and hung loosely over his belt.

"Sorry for the bump, was pushed by someone. Can I buy you another one?" she said.

"Naw," he said as he ushered her up to the bar next to him.

"Let me buy you one, the more you drink the better looking I get." He laughed at his lame joke and put his arm around her. She did not resist. They exchanged the usual get to know each other pleasantries; his natural and hers well-rehearsed. She was Annie Larkin, with a line that she arrived a few months ago from Dublin and now worked as a cleaning lady with the hope of getting a better education and becoming a secretary. When she saw the look on the construction worker's face at the mention of Dublin, she made it clear that she was a Catholic "left footer" and did not care for the Protestant northern Irish. Alcohol and his desire to impress the young lady made him a great conversationalist, and he did most of the talking. She was trained to listen and ask questions, which she did well bringing out a brief history of the man, Kieran Burke, her goal for the evening. Her drinking was measured so as not to cloud her mission, while he imbibed freely. They spoke for over two hours, periodically stepping out on Katonah Avenue for a smoke.

"Glad to have met ya," he slurred as he walked with her to the street level entrance to her apartment. He attempted an awkward kiss while stumbling at the front door. "Would you have me in for a while?"

"Not tonight, but I'd like to see you again, Keiran." Just enough to keep him interested. The rest would come later. "See you at Piper's t'morrow night."

"Awright, awright," he gave a brief bow, and navigated up the street considering a night cap before he retired to his rented room in an overcrowded boarding house, the best he could afford at the time.

Annie Larkin watched him for a while and then disappeared into the alcove.

For the last two months she resided in a small apartment on the second floor of the building at the corner of 236th St. It suited her purposes. She could come and go undetected, and an elderly woman who spent weekends with a relative occupied the only other apartment on her floor. In exchange for these amenities, she put up with the constant odor of butter fried food, which the occupants below her, recently from Ireland used as their culinary staple. She had spent time blending into the neighborhood, washing her clothes at the laundromat a block away and shopping in the local market. She even made herself seen at St. Barnabas Church on Yonkers Ave. attending the noon mass on Sunday.

All this came naturally as she was well schooled, and well experienced in immersing herself into a neighborhood as a regular. She was from Dublin, educated, and knew enough about Kerry and Limerick men to converse with anyone in the neighborhood. MI-5 introduced her to the CIA when her reporting on the IRA became limited, and they felt her talents could be used elsewhere. She considered herself a soldier of fortune, going wherever the money was best. Today, she thought it was the CIA. She had some small assignments in Europe, and was brought to the United States, where she quickly got her green card with the knowledge that it would automatically be extended courtesy of her CIA handler. Eventually, United States citizenship, if she wanted it, would be fast tracked. Her cover as a cleaning lady gave her free access to 147 Park Avenue, a small office building run by the CIA for several covert operations, each compartmentalized in a small interior office. In room 2805 she frequently would be debriefed by Michael Zorn, and receive enough cash in small bills that would exceed her lifestyle.

She usually left her apartment at 7:00 am, and visited different areas of the city, sometimes taking in a movie in the afternoon to absent her from the neighborhood as any working person would. In the evening she stopped briefly in one of the many bars to get a flavor for the local color, and had an occasional conversation with a patron but nothing more. She had found her target at the Piper's Lounge and became a regular.

CHAPTER 4

Freedom Tower site

"Hey Willie, what's up?"

Willie O'Shea, shop steward for Local 18A, looked up as Eddie Michaels walked into the inner office of his plywood shanty on the second floor below street level. O'Shea was in his early sixties, had hands the size of a catcher's mitt, and crusted from many years working with concrete. His red face and large belly reflected years of a bad diet and drink.

"How's the mini Home Depot going?" Michaels was referring to the numerous construction tools that the trade workers signed out and in on a daily basis. They filled the many shelves that rose to the ceiling. Hand grinders, crowbars, power tools, brooms, wrenches, and other items lined dusty shelves. Willie spent most of his time in the inner office going over delivery papers and union matters while an assistant signed out the tools. Copies of the Irish Echo littered his desk, and a dust covered microwave and small refrigerator sat on an upper shelf. Chargers for handheld radios used by the foremen were on another shelf, and winter coats and rain gear hung on nails on the rear wall. Numerous business cards from tool suppliers, and union contacts decorated the side wall.

"It's going very, very well Eddie, sit down." Michaels sat in an old folding chair as Willie leaned back in an old, tattered office chair, removed his reading glasses and pushed the plywood door closed. A Marlboro came from his pocket.

"You're going to die from those things," said Michaels kiddingly. Michaels knew that smoking was prohibited on the site, but never said anything. Willie spoke with a thick coarse brogue; one from his homeland, and the other from years of smoking. He always had a hearty laugh and a good story for visitors.

He took a deep drag on his Marlboro. "A couple more years Eddie, and I can retire. With the overtime I'm making now, I'll have a nice monthly paycheck."

"You keeping the men working?" asked Michaels.

"Aah, you know, we go up and down depending on how quick we catch up with the ironworkers. Averaging around 80 laborers, and expect to increase as the building grows. All our boys passed the background check required by the Port Authority, and are here for the duration."

"Willie, I never knew any Irishman that couldn't pass a background, but there are some I know that couldn't pass a breathalyzer."

"There you go making disparaging remarks about us. And what are you?"

"Me, I'm all Polish. Father's name was Mikulski until he changed it to get work when he came to the country."

"Jesus, want me to start with the Polish jokes? We got a few Polaks in the local."

"Willie, the correct term is Poles. Polak is like calling an Irishman a donkey."

"Call me anything you want, but don't call me late on paydays." Willie gave his hearty laugh. "Ya know Eddie, there is something I wanted to mention to you, but it has to stay between us because I could have everything wrong. I'm just going on my gut feeling, and the guy could just be a weirdo."

"You know everything you say stays between us. What's up?"

"We got a new guy who has been here for about four months now. Kieran Burke. Maurice Daly, our business manager, got him down here because of some calls that came from Kerry. He's a hard worker, but the book on him is that he's a bit of a fuckin' radical. His reputation was that he wanted to rejuvenate the IRA, and professed to be a bomb thrower, although people that knew him say he was basically bullshitting to get attention. I did some checking with some folks in the old country, and it turned out that he spent some time in England, where I was told he hung out with some Muslims. Very fuckin' strange for an Irishman. As you know, we got mostly Irish in our local, but if you look around, we have a few Italians and a couple of Englishmen. All good workers mind you. When we carry rebar or pour concrete, we are all one, and that's the way I have always been. But I almost had to throw this guy Kieran off the site. He got into it with one of our Englishman, Colm Shea, for no reason, and seems to have no pride in what we are doing. Not that he has to be a flag waver."

"That's not much to go on Willie."

"I can't put my finger on it Eddie, but there are little things like making anti-American remarks to the other workers. Nothing threatening, but serious enough for them to bring it to my attention. Like saying the United States is trying to take over the world by the military's involvement in several countries. His disdain for religion. You know most of us are Catholics, and have strong traditions from the old country. Burke made fun of the guys on Ash Wednesday when they came back from noon mass. One thing the Irish don't do is make fun of religion. Also, he smiled when they talked about the underwear bomber last, and remarked that Al-Qaeda had a lot of good points, and maybe a blown-up airplane would wake up capitalistic Americans. I wouldn't mind getting him out of here before there is a real problem, but Maurice wants me to keep him. Says the younger generation is different than we are. Bullshit."

"Get me his green card info, DOB and SSN, and I'll take a look at him. Also, find out what his habits are. What does he do in his spare time? Is he married? If not, does he have a girlfriend? Does he have both? Where does he hang out? Does he drink? I guess the answer to that is yes, he's Irish isn't he?"

"There you go again Eddie. You know the only difference between the Polaks, I mean the Poles, and us, is that they drink vodka, and we drink Irish whiskey and beer. Otherwise, we are the same; Catholics, same history of oppression, freedom fighters and good family men." He winked when he said good family men.

"Willie, it will all be unofficial of course, and you can't mention it to anyone else."

"Eddie, if you knew all the shit I've kept under me fuckin' hat over the years, you'd be surprised. If this looks like anything, I'll do what I can, and even Maurice won't know."

"Thanks Willie. Maybe I can get some excitement back into my job before I retire."

"This old Irishman smells something bad with this guy," said Willie as he dipped his cigarette in a partially filled coffee cup, and rolled it in his fingers above the wastebasket, letting the remnants mix with the rest of the trash.

"They called that field stripping a cigarette when I was in the Marine Corps and had the same bad habit," said Eddie as he was leaving.

"Here they call it covering your ass."

"What's going on Eddie?" Rick Dean, the current head of the FBI's Criminal Division of the New York Office, looked up as Michaels breezed past Dean's administrative assistant, an elderly employee who shot Michaels a look of disdain. Michaels was one of the few who could do that. He worked for Dean when Dean was his supervisor when they brought down the biggest mafia-controlled heroin operation in Harlem. They lived through the murder of an agent, administrative inquiries, and late-night discussions in the bar across from 26 Federal Plaza.

"How's the construction worker doing these days?" Dean knew that Michaels didn't like his assignment, and didn't overdo the kidding.

"Hey, it's not bad. Meet some interesting, hardworking people. The salt of the earth. That's why I'm here."

"Oh Shit. Here we go again." Dean grinned as he leaned back in his executive chair. "What do you need from me now?"

"A favor."

"You see this desk, my chair, and the new mahogany bookcase over there. And include the new car in the basement that came with a driver. They are not even broken in yet, so this favor better not have a hint of me getting my ass into a jam."

"No way. You know I would never ask you

anything that could backfire."

"Go ahead. I can't wait."

"Now that we have dispensed with all the bullshit, here's what I want. I got some confidential information today about an Irish laborer at the Freedom Tower, a guy named Kieran Burke who, in his shop steward's opinion, is a little strange. Appears a little anti-American, is anti-Catholic, and doesn't fit the mold of the typical Irish laborer."

"Eddie, that sounds like half the people who voted for the current administration. Where are you going with this?"

"It's a little more than that. He supposedly has had past contact with Muslim extremists in England, tried to revitalize the old IRA bombings, and doesn't fit in down there."

"Bingo! Who do you work for? Let me answer that – the JTTF. A nice little case for them to look into, and I don't give any favors."

"You know, I could have predicted that answer because I've known you long enough. Here's the predicament. I got this confidentially. This isn't sexy enough for the JTTF to devote any manpower to, so they will just wash it out by interviewing all parties, including my source for all of this and the subject himself. This would knock out any potential conspiracies, if there are any, only to have them rear their head again with some other people."

Dean grinned, "I know what's coming next.

You want my blessing to play around with this under my auspices, and cover your ass if anything blows up in your face. I know you are a stubborn bastard and, although I will deny I ever said this, you did help me move up the administrative ladder by making the big cases.

"This is the deal. We'll open a criminal case in my division under an allegation of the theft of expensive tools from the Freedom Tower. You play around with Burke as the subject. But I warn you, if you come up with anything resembling terrorist activities, you let me know immediately, and I call in JTTF. As the wise guys used to say, Capisce?"

"Capisce."

"Now Eddie, let's get serious. How's Nancy doing?" Michaels went on to discuss his relationship with Nancy Schaeffer and the problems therein as his good friend Dean listened attentively.

CHAPTER 5

The New York Office of the FBI

The day after his meeting with Willie, Michaels had all of the information he needed. Burke's green card was legitimate, his social security number trace showed nothing unusual, and he lived in a boarding house on 139th Street, a block off Katonah Avenue. Single, no known family in the country, liked his Guinness and frequented the Piper's Lounge near his residence. A check of the computerized indices in the office, however, caught Michaels' eye. It was a reference to a file that accumulated miscellaneous information provided by outside sources where there was no substantive violation. The information was only recorded for future reference.

Michaels went to the serial in the file and saw that a Kieran Burke had been under surveillance by Scotland Yard a few years back as a suspect in gunrunning for the IRA and was described by their sources as a hot head who was prone to violence. He also spent some time in England, where he associated with some known Muslim extremists. Nothing came of the matter, but the authorities sent the information to the FBI because Burke had a record of a few trips to the United States. *Good*, thought Michaels, *no mention of terrorism, although that jumps off the page. No need to bring this to the JTTF, and it can stay in the Criminal Division.*

"Dick, how are you doing?" Michaels was happy to catch his old friend on his call to the Pompano Beach condo.

"What could be bad? The eagle shits on the first of every month, I hang at my country club, play golf, and occasionally go to the beach and check out the talent. Are you coming down for a few days? You know I have the second bedroom and even if I have overnight company, that bedroom will be free."

Dick Gerosa was one of the best undercover agents the FBI ever had. After several successful cases, he recently retired out of the New York Office and moved to Florida. A confirmed bachelor, he enjoyed the nightlife, golf and flirting with the ladies.

"You need to settle down Dick or you are going to crash and burn someday," Michaels said kidding.

"Yeah, but what a ride. Now that we have dispensed with the bullshit, how's your new gig going? Just can't imagine you in a hard hat going up and down ladders."

"Good, and that's the reason I'm calling."

"Why, you want a construction job down here? The weather's nice."

"No, Dick – this is serious."

"I'm not into serious anymore, but go ahead. What've you got that you need my advice on?"

"Not your advice Dick, your talent."

"Maybe you don't get the picture Eddie. I'm fat, dumb, happy and retired."

"This will take about a month. We get to hang out like the old days. I'll get you on a per diem consultant rate plus expenses. You just have to play a role and get close to someone."

"Eddie, you know every wise guy in New York knows me after the publicity during the last trial. I couldn't do anything without getting made."

"This is different. It involves the Irish and a possible bad guy who could be a terrorist."

"That's an oxymoron Eddie. No such thing as an Irish terrorist. They only drink and go to church."

"Maybe you never heard of the IRA Dick. When it came to explosives, they were the best. They developed the technique of setting off a bomb and have another one go off as the rescue workers and bystanders came to the scene. It's copied in Iraq and Afghanistan today."

"Let me think about it, I still have a couple of female friends in New York that I have neglected. What will I be doing?"

"Brush up in what you learned when you worked construction while you were going to college."

"Wait a minute, Eddie. I'm not into manual labor. All I know is that it sounds like a Hispanic name."

"You'll be on the business end. Just brush up on the construction terms and how the unions work in New York."

"Let me think about it."

"Bullshit, I'll start the paperwork," said Michaels as he said his goodbye and hung up.

Michaels arranged for a good hourly rate for Gerosa, an apartment in the Pelham Bay section of the Bronx and backstopped his undercover identity through a Long Island contractor who once was a Bureau informant. He would verify that Gerosa, now under the name of Richard Gerardo, worked for him in varying capacities as a foreman, manager, and salesman for the past five years. Gerardo's role would be attempting to get non-union workers to work on several projects that the contractor bid on.

"The apartment's not bad," said Michaels as he checked the bedroom and kitchen. "The only two rooms you'll probably be using. Do you still cook Italian for a hobby?"

"Sure do. But right now, I need to stock the ice box."

"Dick, it is a refrigerator."

"Can't break old habits. It was always an ice box when I grew up."

"I'm leaving you this batch of photos that I took showing the present status of the Freedom Tower, a little history of Local 18A and a picture and background of our target, Kieran Burke. He is the guy I want you to get close to. We did a brief surveillance on him and there are photos of his residence and a bar called the Piper's Lounge where he hangs out. We do not know the woman he's with in the last picture. The surveillance team could only give me so much time. She's probably one of the locals that he picked up.

"Underneath his union credentials is a bit of a radical so if you can show displeasure with our country such as the high taxes you are paying to finance a war, etc., he might open up to you."

"I'll know how to handle him after I speak with him for a few minutes. Remember that I did this before."

Gerosa pulled two Heinekens out of the refrigerator and spread the papers out on the kitchen table.

"I'll look at all this later. Right now, let's enjoy a few beers."

47

CHAPTER 6

Gate 1A, Vesey Street entrance to the Freedom Tower

Gerosa spent the last three hours observing the construction workers from outside the gate. Entrance was gained only after the security guard scanned a worker's pass into his hand-held device, and it blinked green and produced a photo to show that the bearer was who he purported to be, and had clearance to enter the site. This was Gerosa's third day of pacing about, and he hoped that he had been noticed on the two previous days. The smokers came out on schedule to finish off lunch with a cigarette, while others sat against the corner building and took some sun. Others ogled at the passing beauties.

Those not scheduled for overtime began to exit, some heading to the nearby subway station, and some directly to one of the local watering holes where they would down a ball and a beer before traveling further. He finally spotted Burke, a loner who took the subway to the Bronx. Burke would wait until he got to the Piper's Lounge before he downed his Guinness.

"Hey man, wanna talk to you." Burke was surprised by Gerosa, dressed in a pair of chino work pants and a blue short-sleeved shirt. His left breast pocket had a couple of pens and some business cards. Typical garb for a business agent or a small-time contractor.

"What d'ya want?" Burke stopped and curiously eyed Gerosa.

"Here's my card." Gerosa removed one of the cards from the Long Island contractor that had the name Richard Gerardo printed on it with the title of superintendent. Burke studied it for a moment.

"What's that got to do with me?"

"My company is bidding on a few new jobs. Not like this one where all eyes are on you. They are nonunion jobs, and we can even avoid paying the prevailing wage. That translates to a low bid if we can get laborers to come in on a cash basis. It won't interfere with what you are doing here. Some nights and weekends, and cash at the end of the shift. Call it found money. No taxes taken out. You've probably done it before, and if you haven't, I can name half a dozen guys who came out the gate during the last ten minutes who did work for me. They would never admit it because they don't want their business agent to find out they're doing nonunion work. If you come with me on a part time basis, no one will know, and if you happen to know the person you are working alongside of, be assured both of you will forget the other is there."

"What kind of work, and how much an hour?"

Gerosa noted Burke's interest, and decided to come in with a nonnegotiable rate slightly above the standard nonunion job.

"You will be doing deconstruction initially, clean up, some cement work, and probably some mason tending. Twenty-five bucks an hour. I got guys lined up for this, but they are mostly Hispanics. Don't know if they are here legally or who the hell they are. I'm Italian, but I like the way you Irish guys work, and if you are working down here," Gerosa gestured towards the Freedom tower, "I know you are here legitimately, and haven't been collared."

Burke studied the business card for a moment.

"I'll let ya know. Is that your cell phone on the card?"

"You got it. By the way, where you going?" Gerosa was ready to reel in his catch.

"Bronx. Katonah Ave. area. You familiar with it?"

"Yup. Did some jobs in that area. I'm from Pelham Bay. My car's down the street. I'll give you a ride, and you can buy me a beer. "I'm Italian, but maybe I could pass for Irish if I don't open me mouth." Gerosa accented the "me mouth" in a phony Irish brogue. "In fact, I have a cooler in the car, and we can have one for the ride."

"Aw fuck it." Burke looked at the card to get the name right. "Dick – who can resist a ride and a beer?"

They walked to the corner, and got into Gerosa's undercover vehicle, a year-old black GMC Sierra truck. He removed a NYC Department of Buildings parking plaque that Michaels made up for him, from the dashboard.

"Got it from a friend of mine in the Building Department." Gerosa grinned as Burke took it all in, believing that Gerosa was a guy that had contacts.

They drove talking mainly about construction with Gerosa zeroing in on Burke's roots in Ireland with the hope of getting into his persona. Years of undercover work made Gerosa a pro, and when they pulled onto Katonah Avenue, he knew almost as much as he had to. Gerosa played the "I'm disgusted with America because they take all my money in taxes, which are going to support a war against rag heads that I don't give a shit about."

This caught a bit of Burke's attention. He was reluctant to delve into his inner feelings, but agreed with Gerosa along the way. They popped open their second Bud as they worked their way across the Cross Bronx, and onto the Deegan Expressway to the 233rd St. exit that led to Katonah Ave. There they made a left into the line of Irish restaurants and bars.

"We're two blocks away, park anywhere on the street. The meters will be legal in another hour, but no one'll bother you now," said Burke. Gerosa pulled into a spot near the Piper's Lounge and shunned the parking meter. What did he care, he wouldn't pay for it anyway. Michaels would get the tab.

It was only 4:00 pm, but the Piper's was jumping. Some were on unemployment, some on workman's comp, some home early from work, and some too lazy to go to work that day. Irish tunes were playing on the jukebox, and Irish football on the television had the attention of those who had bet on the game.

"Two Guinness," Burke directed the bartender.

"You have to try a Guinness. They pour the best here of any bar on Katonah Avenue. It'll grow on you." Gerosa had a few in the past, didn't care for the heaviness, but decided to play along.

"I said I would buy," said Gerosa as he dropped a fifty on the bar. This caught the attention of the bartender as well as Burke. Fifties were not common in the Piper's. "Sláinte!" said Burke as he raised his pint. "That's the same as Cheers in Gaelic,"

"Cent' Anni," said Gerosa as he did likewise. "That means you should live for a hundred years."

"Not at my job," Burke said, "After years of working with concrete you either get back problems or bad feet from walking over the rebar before a pour."

They had two, and two led to three. Burke now felt comfortable with Gerosa, and began to talk about his time in Ireland, and how fearless he was in taking on the Brits with the IRA.

"What religion are you?" he asked Gerosa.

"Was a Catholic, but the priest scandals pissed me off, so now I am nothing." Gerosa didn't know where Burke was going with this. He knew about the IRA, but wanted more information regarding Burke's sojourn to England and his involvement with the Muslims.

"Me too, but the pedophile shit was worse than ever in Ireland. I gave up long ago." Burke was going to mention his Muslim contacts, but decided his tongue was getting too loose. "Fuck it. All religions suck. Let's talk about the job again."

"Give me your cell number, and I will get in touch with you. How soon are you available?" Gerosa took down the number as an attractive young female approached them at the bar. They were now into their third hour, and weren't counting their beers. Gerosa was bloated but wanted to keep up with Burke.

"And what might you be doin' here, and who is your friend?" Annie Larkin stepped between the two. Burke introduced Gerosa and ordered another Guinness.

"Did you forget our dinner date?" Larkin folded her arms in mock annoyance.

"No, we'll leave after this beer."

Gerosa saw another opportunity. "Why don't we all go to dinner, I'm buying. Never had really good Irish food. Got a place nearby?"

Larkin and Burke nodded in agreement.

The remainder of the evening was spent at Rory Dolan's restaurant on Yonkers Avenue, where they all ordered Dublin style fish and chips. The small conversation continued with Gerosa randomly interjecting questions, the answers to which would give him a better picture of the two. Two Irish coffees finished the meal.

"Dinner was a good change for me. Are you guys interested in some good Italian food sometime? Some nice veal parm, snapper Livornese, or chicken cacciatore? I got the place," Gerosa said. Burke and Larkin glanced at each other, and nodded in agreement.

"Good. Call and let me know what day is good for you. And let me know about the job I'm offering you. You got my number on the card."

On the way back to his apartment in Pelham Bay, Gerosa went over the day's conversation with Burke, which he would reduce to writing when he arrived. Nothing jumped out at him, but his undercover experience gave him an uneasy feeling.

Burke and Larkin had been sleeping together for over a month, and they went directly to her apartment where she turned on the television, which ran continuously when they were there. She had started to execute her suggestive behavior plan as outlined by Zorn. MSNBC and Chris Matthews regularly ranted against republicans, and those with money, and how there was inequality in the distribution of wealth, the present talking points of liberal politicians.

"Look at all the money being spent in Afghanistan killing innocent people. Look how many rich people are there while others starve. Only the rich get to go to a good college. Why is the United States interfering with foreign governments? Bankers are as crooked here as they are in Ireland," and so on she repeated regularly.

She got him into discussing his sympathetic views toward extremists. The opportune time was during their regular watching where the host was decrying a U. S. errant drone attack that landed on a schoolhouse in Afghanistan. A film clip of the Taliban waving automatic weapons with dead children as the backdrop followed.

"Sometimes I wonder why I ever came here," she said as forced tears rolled down her cheeks. She could feel his anger mounting, and as she repeated her statement, he jumped out of bed and walked towards the television. "Fuckin' Americans. Fuckin' Americans." He shook his head and walked into the kitchen to fetch a beer.

He did not realize that he was being manipulated, and that the end game was to his own detriment. Her plan was to subvert his sense of control over his decision-making process, and it had begun. It was easier than she thought because the seeds for irrational conduct already had been sown when he was in England.

For another hour, they commiserated with the plight of America's enemies, and she would occasionally suggest some kind of violence in retribution. He shrugged it off at first, but she was persuasive, using her sexual prowess and alcohol to elicit statements he would not normally make. Soon, every night they discussed some kind of retribution against the Americans right where they lived. When she moved from persuasive to authoritative, he seemed to go along. It started when her suggestions turned to definitive statements.

"Something has to be done" replaced "What do you think should be done. We have to do something" replaced "What can we do?" She could tell he was gradually moving from passive to passive-aggressive, and eventually to fully aggressive, which is where she wanted him. Then Zorn would give her the specifics, which thus far were kept from her. This didn't bother her as long as she continued to receive her weekly stipend, and believed that she was working for the CIA with the full authority of the U. S. government behind her.

During the next two weeks, Burke worked one weekend with the contractor contact on Long Island. He had a few jobs going on, and was able to work in Burke with the other laborers that worked for him, the bargaining point being that the Bureau would pay his wages. Burke, Larkin and Gerosa had dinner again, and they continued usually once a week. They went to Italian restaurants in Little Italy, Chinese in Chinatown, and steaks at a local steakhouse all on Gerosa, or rather the FBI's dime.

Gerosa kept the political discussions going.

"Look at this current administration. This new healthcare bill will stop my boss from hiring additional workers; that is if he went legitimate and paid out a regular paycheck with all the deductions."

Gerosa had to carefully weave this in so as not to offend the unions that Burke believed in because they got him his paycheck at the Freedom Tower.

"You're right Dick," Burke said several times during the most recent dinner at The Rambling House on Katonah Avenue. The bantering about the government's shortcomings amused Larkin. She looked at it as nothing more than additional encouragement to get Burke to do her bidding, albeit something she was not privy to at the time.

"I need a smoke," said Burke as he headed for the door on this particular evening while waiting for coffee and shots of Jameson's.

"I'll join you," Larkin said as she reached for the smokes in her purse. She followed him out while Gerosa remained at the table. As soon as they were outside, Gerosa grabbed Larkin's purse and rummaged through it quickly. He grabbed her wallet first and checked the cards. Two hundred dollars, no driver's license, a green card, and a Medicaid card. Nothing unusual. He flipped her cell phone open, and quickly memorized the number. He then went to her call log. Nothing. Either she didn't make calls or erased them immediately. He thought that strange. Two hundred dollars didn't compute with her job as a cleaning lady either.

CHAPTER 7

New York FBI Office

Eddie Michaels was summoned to Rick Dean's office, and he surmised that having Gerosa play around with Burke was coming to an end, and he was prepared. He took his position in one of the easy chairs at the far end of the room. A coffee table separated him and Dean, who occupied a similar chair facing him. Dean would never have his friend sit facing his oak desk as he would a subordinate.

"Okay, Eddie. Give me a really good reason to continue this quest of yours started by an Irishman at the Freedom Tower. I don't think any more money will be forthcoming from headquarters, and the charade that this is an investigation into the theft of tools is wearing thin."

"I would have come in sooner, but I just received the information that I was looking for." He leaned back in his chair and played a little game with his old friend, who knew exactly what he was doing.

"Stop the bullshit games Eddie, I know you got something on your mind."

"You've been getting daily emails from me, and you know that Gerosa has established a good rapport with Burke and his girlfriend, and you can read between the lines that this guy is not your patriotic, religious, flag waving Irishman."

"That doesn't make him a terrorist."

"Something funny is going on here and it's not funny ha ha. Let me give you the latest chapter. The other night Gerosa was able to get the number for Annie Larkin's cell phone. I called our mutual friend and former agent, Joe Groghan, over at Verizon. Luckily, Larkin has a Verizon account and Groghan gave me the details of her last month's calls. I know, I know, we are supposed to have a subpoena, so forget I'm telling you this. Also, none of this will come to a courtroom. There was one number that was called almost on a daily basis, a cell phone that also had a Verizon account. The subscriber is Goldstone Consultants, 147 Park Avenue. Does that ring a bell?'

Dean leaned forward. "Goldstone means nothing, but the address surely does. I remember a year ago we had a sensitive operation using a CIA operative and we learned that the Park Avenue address was their cover for domestic covert operations although they are not supposed to do anything domestically. If I recall, they had the three floors from the top to enhance their communications system and satellite tracking."

"I checked Goldstone, and they are on the 38th floor. The building has forty floors. Bingo. I even called the number under pretext and got a generic recording to leave a message. One more tidbit – during Gerosa's dealings with Burke and Larkin, he discreetly asked a million questions, and learned that Larkin is a cleaning lady, and her main customers are on Park Avenue. He didn't push for the exact address." Michaels smiled and leaned back in his chair.

"Stop with the shit eating grin," Dean said as he stared at nothing in particular on the wall behind Michaels. "Sounds like a CIA operation, but why the hell would they be interested in Burke. And who the hell is Larkin, except maybe an asset? I think it is time to turn this over to the JTTF and let them deal with the CIA."

"Rick, let this play out a little longer. We only have half a story. If we go to the CIA now, they will cover their tracks pretty well and come up with some plausible explanation."

"What do you suggest?"

"Let's find out who Larkin is contacting. We have the cell phone number, and the tech people can pinpoint her location at any given time. Let's run it for a week, and if there is a pattern, we can spot check one of the locations and take the guy to wherever and try to identify him."

"And where, might I ask, do we go for the

resources to do this? We've got a full plate here."

"Extend Gerosa for another month and he and I will handle it."

"What's the matter, he didn't make all his female contacts in the month he was here," Dean said half-jokingly. "And what about your job at the Freedom Tower?"

"Shit, they won't even miss me. I don't have to do daily reports and besides, they think that I am down there pre-retirement and am doing very little anyway. "

"I'll give you one more shot to come up with something, but in the meantime, I will have to go to the boss of the JTTF, who is my counterpart, and let him know what is going on. I'll downplay the whole thing because I know they are interested in anyone from the Mideast and probably couldn't care less about a drunken Irishman. I won't say anything about the possible CIA connection until we know more."

"Sounds good to me," Michaels said, "I know Dick will be happy because he is now into this whole gig, and like me, he believes there is more to the story than the story."

"Do me a favor and come back with the old Paul Harvey saying: 'Now you know the rest of the story."

Later that day, Dean called Michaels. "You have the green light from the JTTF. As I predicted they have their hands full with foreign and homegrown terrorists and kind of laughed me out of the room when I mentioned an Irishman. The boss there is Brian Donovan, and he would refuse to believe that any Irishman would be a terrorist. He suggested that you have your contact at the Freedom Tower, who started this whole thing, go to Alcoholics Anonymous. Thanks. I got the tech guys on board to track the phone, and with the equipment they now have it is almost like automatic pilot. I'll have them run the phone for a week and see what happens."

Gerosa continued his once-a-week dinners with Burke and Larkin probing more into Burke's politics; the problem being that it took several Guinness to get him talking. And then he became almost irrational, cursing the British and the American political system. Michaels kept to restaurants where they poured Guinness or at least had Jameson at the bar to keep Burke fueled with his favorites. After dinner and full of drinks, Gerosa always tried to push Burke a little further.

"What can we do about it?" he would ask or "How do we stop this?" to get into his head, and the response was always "Nothin', fuckin' nothing right now." Gerosa always used "we" hoping to get into whatever Burke was planning. He avoided this in Larkin's presence because he didn't know much about her except that she was contacting the CIA and that was not good. The truth that at this time in the chain of events, Burke knew very little. His moment would come as the September 11 memorial drew closer. Frustrated at his lack of immediate success with Burke, Gerosa was developing a plan to get to Larkin.

Although he had a liberal expense account, Gerosa preferred practicing his culinary skills at his apartment and this evening, he made osso buco and the smell of fresh garlic filled the air. He just brought it to a simmer on the stove as Michaels entered, a bottle of Chianti in one hand and his briefcase in the other. The small apartment, previously used to video and wiretap a mobster who lived down the street, met Gerosa's needs except for the kitchen. He bought some new utensils and stocked the cabinet with spices. Fresh parsley and oregano were in the refrigerator. On the countertop was an ample supply of olive oil and fresh garlic.

"Smells good," said Michaels as he dropped his briefcase on a kitchen chair and gave the wine to Gerosa for opening.

"Must have spent a few bucks on this. It has a cork, not a screw top." Gerosa opened the bottle and poured two glasses. See those small spoons on the table. I bought them especially for this meal. You use them to scrape the marrow out of the veal shank. Best part of the meal." Gerosa gave a wink and a wolfish grin as he removed the ever-present dishcloth that he slung over his shoulder while he cooked.

"Let's see what we have." He pulled up a chair

as Michaels removed some computer printouts from his briefcase.

Michaels briefed Gerosa on the week's calls from Larkin's cell phone to the cell phone subscribed to by a vague business in the same building and on the same floor as covert CIA locations.

"Before we go over these, I got you a month extension. Also, the JTTF shows no interest in the Irishman, so the ball is in my court. Take a look at these computer printouts because we are going to have to first of all, identify the guy Larkin is calling. I've highlighted the pattern that he follows during the day. His cell phone includes GPS chips, which can determine his location and is mainly used for 911 emergencies. Normally, the phone company will charge an extra twenty-five bucks for this service if someone wants it to track their kids or for commercial use to track employees like truck drivers. Our tech guys can do it without the phone company knowing. Looking at the chart, you will see that the GPS puts him at Bell Road in Scarsdale in the evening and in the early morning so we can assume that that is where he lives. It pinpoints the house at number 25 near the corner of Brook St. and Hylan Blvd. I'm having our analysts do a workup on the residents of that house as well as the ones next door and a couple across the street in case the GPS is off. Hopefully, we can ID our guy.

"It's all residential. Then he is all over the

place. What is really interesting is that on Thursday, whoever it is, is in the FBI office at 26 Fed around nine forty-five in the morning. Left around eleven thirty. What I came up with is that there was a Homeland Security briefing in the Assistant Director's conference room from ten to eleven. If our guy was there, I thought he would have to have been the CIA rep. I checked on the attendees who represented about every law enforcement and regulatory agency known to man, about twenty-five total, and there were two reps from the CIA. One is a high-ranking female and the other the second in command of the New York station. They both live in New Jersey. He's about sixty-five and has been there his whole career. She is a rising star right out of their Washington headquarters. Neither makes any sense.

"Let's connect the dots. Burke was looked at briefly by MI-5 because of his IRA connections and some contacts in England with extremists. Nothing came of it, but they alerted the Bureau because of Burke's travel to the States, and nothing was done here because he was not important."

"Interesting," said Gerosa. "Keep going, this is almost as exciting as sex."

Michaels stopped for a moment and looked up. "I doubt it in your case."

Michaels continued, "When I saw a copy of the letter that they sent to headquarters, the copy count included the CIA. So, we presume that they forwarded the letter to their New York station just as headquarters sent the letter to the New York Office. Based on the Bureau's lack of interest and the lack of facts in the letter indicating that Burke was a threat, I imagine that the CIA did just what the Bureau did. File the letter and forget about it. So why is Annie Larkin calling someone in the CIA?"

Gerosa interrupted. "You're assuming that she is calling someone in the CIA because the subscriber comes back to a location we believe is used by the CIA for covert reasons. Do we know anything about Goldstone Consultants?"

"Nothing. Just a bullshit name. No website, nothing on the Internet or any Better Business Bureau or any corporate records. The phone company has the name Walter Smith, which is probably also bogus, as the contact at the billing address. We could assume that she is calling her CIA contact and is an informant or what they politely call an asset. If so, what the hell is she doing? You've been out with her, and she is basically an emigrant from Ireland who hooked up with Burke. Is Burke more important than he was made out to be? His background doesn't warrant a covert CIA operative getting close to him. Maybe a little quirky in the way he behaves, but certainly not a threat.

Gerosa agreed with him. "He talks crazy sometimes, but usually after a few drinks. Aside from disliking the current administration, the war in Afghanistan and mostly everything the government is into overseas, he has not shown any affinity towards radical Islam or Muslim extremists. Maybe I can try and drag something out of him regarding his time in England during one of our dinners, or better more, maybe it would be better if I catch him alone without Larkin." Michaels nodded in agreement.

Their attention was again riveted to the printouts. "See this," said Michaels as he pointed to a highlighted item. On Sunday at around nine in the morning, he drives to Wyndham in upstate New York, stays there until about three in the afternoon and drives back. The coordinates on the GPS show nothing on a map. It is either farmland, or a remote hunting lodge. There are several up there. I tried Google Earth, but all I saw were trees in the general area. Our analyst should be back tomorrow to see if she can make anything out of this. Wait a minute, I've got an idea." Michaels scrolled through the names on his cell phone and rang one up.

"Rick, are the special ops flyboys doing anything tomorrow?" he asked Rick Dean, who picked up on the second ring.

"From what I recall, they have two fixed wing aircraft and two helicopters stashed in some small airport in New Jersey under a fictitious name. I'd like to take an early morning ride upstate to those GPS coordinates and see what is there."

"Now you are pushing it. Not a bad idea

though. Let me call Joe Hannigan and see if he needs some hours in the helicopter. He can even pick us up at the west side heliport."

"Rick, forget about the us. Dick and I work better without adult supervision and, not to be disrespectful, I don't want you fucking this whole thing up."

Dean knew he was kidding about fucking up their trip, and also knew that Michaels did not want him around for whatever they had in mind if they found something. He agreed not to go.

CHAPTER 8

An upstate helicopter ride

The sky was clear as the Bell Jet Ranger helicopter stopped briefly at the heliport to pick up its passengers. They exchanged greetings with Hannigan, a friend who always went out his way to accommodate them. In a few minutes they moved up the Hudson River, a thousand feet above the water at 140 miles per hour. Michaels sat in the copilot's seat, Gerosa in the rear. Joe Hannigan gave a running account of New York landmarks as they passed the Bear Mountain Bridge, and banked left over the stone structures of the military academy at West Point.

"Diverted from the direct route," said Hannigan. "Thought you might want to see where I went to school. After that, Officers Training, then flight school. Next stop Iraq where I'm lucky I didn't get my ass shot off. Good experience though. Wouldn't trade for the grunts on the ground.

"We'll now cross the New York Thruway, and bear west over some of the Catskills. Nice scenery, so enjoy it. I have the coordinates plugged into this bird, and it should take us right over the mysterious spot in the woods."

Gerosa was getting queasy as the chopper bumped around a little when they faced a side wind. "How long do you figure?" he asked in a tone that gave away his rolling stomach.

"About another 20 minutes. If you have to puke, there is a bag back there, but rather than dirty my bird, I'd rather set down on any open space that we can. I'll try and keep her steady.

"Well, look at that. Right on schedule." Hannigan was lowering the chopper towards a stone cabin masked by trees about a quarter mile off a dirt road. According to the map, it was a mile west of the Windham Country Club, and exclusive country club in Greene County. He banked, and circled clockwise so that Gerosa and Michaels could get a good look.

"See that open spot on the right? I can tell by the way that the grass is blown away, and the brush cut that this was made to order for us to land if you want. Someone has been here in a chopper before, and not long ago. What do you think? I don't see any cars in the area. Closest spot is the golf club, and they won't pay any attention to us, particularly if there has been a chopper in and out of here before. If anyone comes out, I can say that an engine light went on, and I wanted to check."

"Make it quick," said Gerosa. Michaels laughed. "Big tough undercover guy getting sick. Can't wait to spread that around."

"Fuck you – get this thing down."

Hannigan came in fast and raised the front of the chopper to slow it, and then gently dropped to the center of the cleared area.

"Hey Dick, on the way home I'll go through our autorotation drill where I shut the engine off and start it again after it auto rotates down a bit. I was going to do it unannounced on the way up here, but I didn't want you shitting your pants."

Gerosa didn't answer, but bolted to the woods from the craft as soon as it touched down. He returned a few minutes later. Hannigan and Michaels were out of the craft, and were waiting for him."

"Enough with the grins," Gerosa said as he too was grinning.

"It's your show," said Hannigan. "I'm only the chauffeur."

"Then you see nothing from this point on," said Michaels. He turned towards Gerosa. "You bring the picks?" referring to lock picks, a set of which Gerosa had from when he went to tech school to learn phone taps and lock picking.

"Sure did. But first of all, let's check the windows and the doors to make sure that no one is there, and also that there is no easy way in such as an open window. You go around to the left, and I'll check the right side.

Hannigan whistled, and rolled his eyes to the sky. "Why didn't I know something like this was going to happen with you two guys?"

Gerosa and Michaels were very meticulous as they checked the perimeter of the cabin. It was old stone and rustic with a slate roof and two chimneys. Inside were two bedrooms and two baths and a large living room with two fireplaces. Windows were few, and were recently installed to provide better insulation. There was no way they could be opened. Michaels and Gerosa met at the rear of the cabin.

"No easy way in," said Gerosa. "I'll see if I still have my skills, depending on the type of lock they have on the front door." They moved to the front covering their tracks in the dirt around the perimeter separating the cabin from the woods. Gerosa studied the Schlage dead bolt lock, and then rummaged through a small kit that he took from what looked like a briefcase, but was a compartmentalized toolbox. Selecting the right tension bar and rake, he began his work as Michaels went back to sit in the chopper where Hannigan was studying the latest maintenance manual. "He'll be awhile. Not like the movies where the good guys are in with a few strokes of a rake."

A half hour later, Gerosa shouted "Done."

Michaels joined him at the entrance where they took off their shoes and donned cloth slippers and latex gloves before entering. "Just make sure that you put anything back that you touch," Gerosa cautioned Michaels. "Done this before," was Michaels' response.

Gerosa put his hand back to halt Michaels. "Wait until I clear the room for any motion detector alarm systems. There was none on the door, so I don't expect any, but I want to play it safe." His eyes scanned the large living room, and after a brief walk of the perimeter, he motioned Michaels to move forward. Gerosa was busy opening drawers and closets for anything to identify its occupants. He and Michaels knew that an open inquiry with the town would surely get back to the owner, which is the last thing they wanted. Michaels found nothing of interest in the living room, and was sitting on the couch when he noticed some magazines in a rack between the couch and the end table. He grabbed a few of what appeared to be trade magazines, and thumbed through them when the addressee of the subscriber caught his attention: Coordinated Technologies, 25 Executive Boulevard, Rye, New York, Suite 603. Inside, it promoted the latest developments in armament produced by the major countries of the world. Another showed the latest development in radar and technical equipment. Michaels used his cell phone to take pictures of what he considered magazines of interest, all sent to Coordinated Technologies.

Gerosa walked out of the bedroom holding copies of legal papers submitted by both sides in a criminal case that appeared to be under appeal. The documents were all addressed to the Honorable Robert Kirkland, the judge hearing the case in the Southern District of New York federal courthouse in downtown New York's Foley Square.

"Very God damn interesting," muttered Gerosa as he sat next to Michaels on the couch as he flipped through the documents.

"Take a look at this." Michaels spread copies of the tech magazines on the coffee table. "Strange bedfellows." He grabbed his cell phone and hit the speed dial. It was the direct line to Patty Brady, an intelligence analyst assigned to the criminal division under Dean. Michaels avoided the JTTF analyst in the event the pieces added up to terrorism, and he knew that Brady did not discuss her work with anyone.

"Patty, Eddie here. What did you find re the GPS locations?"

"I was about to call you because this is interesting. I ran backgrounds on the occupants of all the nearby Scarsdale homes, and they are all benign except one, Michael Zorn. Not too much came up except he is a government employee. I figured that if he lives in Scarsdale, he must be somewhere at the top of the GS levels, a 13 or above. I played around with Google and saw that there was a Michael Zorn who was appointed to the position of Homeland Security adviser for the State of New York by the governor and had a background with the CIA. Next, I checked our own indices and saw that Zorn is a regular attendee at the Homeland Security conference we host every couple of months. So, he is your guy."

"Many thanks, Patty. One more favor. See what you can find on Coordinated Technologies in Rye, New York, and federal judge Robert Kirkland." Michaels shut off his phone and related his conversation to Gerosa who was scanning through the magazines.

"I don't know what we are getting ourselves into," said Michaels. "Let's head back, and digest what we have and try to see where we are going." Michaels placed the magazines back in the same order that he removed them, and Gerosa moved towards the bedroom to return the legal papers to their original position.

"I'll meet you at the chopper," said Gerosa.

Michaels stopped momentarily as if to ask a question, but grinned and headed for the door. Moments later Gerosa emerged from the bedroom, and again surveyed the living room. He moved to the couch, stood for a few moments, and then sat, his eyes still searching. They finally fixed on the coffee table, and he grinned as he dropped to his knees, and looked at the underside. *Perfect*, he thought. He again went to his briefcase and removed a small device, the size of a cigarette box, from one of the compartments. Next came a few pieces of double-sided tape to which he affixed the voice activated digital recorder. Again, looking under the coffee table, he found a smooth surface behind the molding that ran the perimeter of the table, and extended three inches below the top. He hit the on switch, and the tiny red light signaled that it was now on. It had twenty-four hours of battery life used up only when someone's voice activated it. He stuck it on the underside of the table.

On his way out, Gerosa stopped at the front door, and again went to his briefcase. Another set of tools came out, and he methodically dismantled the door's locking mechanism. With the precision of a surgeon, he took apart the lock cylinder, and removed all but two of the pins. He went through a set of blank keys that also came out of his briefcase and found one with a similar keyway as the lock. He punched slots in the key to match the two remaining pins in the lock, reassembled the lock and smiled when the key that he made worked perfectly. He checked around him, and smoothed out the dirt near the door where he had walked.

Hannigan had already warmed up the chopper and started the rotor moving when he saw Gerosa leaving the house, and grinned when he got in. "I see nuzzing, hear nuzzing, and say nuzzing," imitating Sergeant Schultz from the television series Hogan's Heroes. I am just your humble chauffeur. I presume we will be returning here."

"Not necessarily," said Michaels, "We can drive up here in the future now that we know what we have. For the record, you took us on a sightseeing tour today because you needed the hours, and wanted to show Gerosa the countryside."

"I'm way ahead of you. It is already in my logbook. I even put in that we landed in an open area because Dick got sick to his stomach, and I didn't want to dirty my bird." Hannigan turned the throttle, and increased the pitch on the rotor as he guided the chopper up and out. They made small talk as they returned, but nothing more was said of the last two hours.

CHAPTER 9

Wyndham hunting lodge

Zorn, Whitaker, and Kirkland sat around a coffee table at their regular upstate meeting. Zorn had arrived by car, and Kirkland and Whitaker's helicopter pilot had since departed. Zorn was attending to his laptop as he made small conversation. The laptop came to life, and he placed it on the table. He raised his head, indicating that he was ready for business.

Kirkland began. "A month ago, you talked about suggestive behavior and mind control, and that Burke would be the pawn of your asset in a few weeks. What progress has been made? Can we be sure that he will do her bidding when the time comes?"

Whitaker nodded in agreement.

"I want you to take a look at this," said Zorn as he turned his laptop on the coffee table, facing it towards Kirkland and Whitaker, and moved his chair to the side, so they all could see the screen.

His presentation was ready to go. Kirkland and Whitaker leaned forward as Zorn started a video.

"The first part is to give you a picture of who I am dealing with. The camera is hidden in the standing lamp to the side of the television set, and focused on the couch. That she is dressed scantily, and appears to exude sex has nothing to do with what Burke is about to do." There was no reaction or questions, so Zorn moved the cursor to the play icon.

The clear color video started by showing Larkin and Burke seated on the couch, her in a half open bathrobe, and he in his boxer shorts. They were watching the late MSNBC news, and commenting back and forth about the U.S. policies in the Mideast. The audio from the television could be heard in the background.

"There is a mike in the back of the couch that overrides the television," said Zorn, "Notice how the conversation gravitates to antipathy towards our government whenever an international story is broadcast. This scene is usually replayed every night before they go to bed, but for tonight, I gave her specific instructions. They both had a few beers at the local pub, he more than her, but be assured that he is not acting in a drunken stupor in what you are about to see. "

"Continue," said the judge with a bit of annoyance knowing that Zorn was stringing him on. MSNBC was on, and a segment showing a recent drone attack on a village in Afghanistan was being reported.

"I wonder how many children died in that attack," asked Larkin, "and more important, how many women and children are killed in attacks that are not reported?"

Burke shook his head in disbelief and grimaced. "I feel that I should go back to England or France and join one of the movements in the Muslim community. I've been there before. Maybe Somalia for training. If it wasn't for the money, I would not be working at the Freedom Tower. It should be called the capitalists' tower because it is only there to make money so the government can rule the world at the cost of the poor. "

Larkin placed her hand on his knee and leaned towards his ear. "You are more important right where you are. There's a reason that you are giving me updates on the progress, and loading my computer with pictures taken from your cell phone. If you think it is idle curiosity on my part? It is not. There is something that I might ask you to do in the future that is better than joining any cause, but I have to know if you have the stomach for it."

"What are ya talking about? You know my feelings towards you, and my hate for the system here. Tell me what I got to do."

"First, I have to see if you have the guts. Are you willing to take chances?"

"For you, and for what I believe in, yeah. I've done shit before that you don't know about where I've put my ass on the line." There was no questioning Burke's tone.

He was positive and straightforward. No hesitancy.

The video continued as Larkin was about to test her time spent at suggestive behavior. She left the room and returned shortly holding a .38 caliber chief special five shot revolver.

"Let me see how much of a risk taker you claim to be." She looked at him and grinned. She had Burke's full attention with the sight of the gun.

"What the fuck are ya doin' with that thing?" His serious moment then changed.

"Aw, stop fuckin' around with that pea shooter. I've handled bigger things than that. Gimme that thing before you hurt yourself." Burke was now grinning.

"Never knew you had that in the house." He reached for the gun, but she pulled back.

"Not so fast. I want you to prove something to me."

"Ah shit. Okay, I'll play your fuckin' game." He leaned back on the couch.

Larkin remained silent as she opened the cylinder, spun it, and inserted one round in a chamber and snapped it shut. She handed the gun to Burke, hand grip towards him, her hand covering the front of the cylinder so the position of the bullet in the chamber could not be seen.

"Take it Kieran. Aim it at the side of your head. Pull the trigger. Do you have the balls to take a chance? If not, I think you are full of shit with all of your political rhetoric."

Burke became serious. "You're not shittin' me, are ya? Gimme the fuckin' gun."

Kirkland and Whitaker moved closer to the laptop, unsure of what they would be witnessing. "Relax," said Zorn, "the bullet she inserted is a dummy shell." They returned to their positions.

Burke took the gun from her hands, held it against the right side of his head, and immediately pulled the trigger without flinching.

"Is that good enough, woman? Don't ever accuse me of not having any balls when it comes to doin' what you want me to do. We are good together. Whatever you want, you got fer shit's sake."

"Again?" he asked as he started to raise the gun to his head again." She grabbed his hand, leaned over, and kissed him. "No Kieran. Sorry that I even doubted you. There is a lot for us to do in the near future."

"Who are you working for?" asked Burke. "Is it another country, a radical group here in the states, some political group or just a bunch of crazies? I won't just do things for anyone or anything. Only against what I know is wrong. I just want to make sure that you'll be safe, and will be there for me."

"You will find out in time and will be surprised to see that you have the opportunity to go down in history," she said. "You don't have to know any more for the time being." Larkin turned toward him and started to move her right hand up the inside of his thigh.

Zorn hit the pause and then the exit icon and closed the cover. "The rest of the video is irrelevant and so your prurient imaginations don't run wild, all she does is get him aroused and then leads him into the bedroom like a pull toy. I might add that this was all accomplished within a few weeks. No drugs were involved although, if necessary, a small amount of LSD could be used to see if it would enhance the control she has over him. There have been experiments that show LSD is effective in mind control as well as all its adverse effects, but right now repetition and basic sex seem to work."

"Very impressive. Is there a camera in the bedroom also?" asked Whitaker as he grinned.

"Please, let's keep this on a professional level." Kirkland appeared annoyed at Whitaker's attempt at levity. "What floor are we up to?"

"We are at the 60th floor. Not really the 60th, but it jumps after the 6th floor to the 20th, reason being that the first six floors have mezzanines and higher ceilings, but they are the equivalent of 24 floors. I get daily briefings from my asset, along with pictures that she downloads from Burke's phone camera and then emails to me. Originally, he thought that she was keeping a pictorial history of the construction for a future book, but as you see from the video, he now knows that it is more than that."

'How can we be sure that his curiosity won't cause him to go outside our little circle?" asked Whitaker.

"We don't. But if we find out that he does, he can easily disappear, and we go back to square one."

"We can't afford that," said Kirkland.

"Don't worry, that will never happen," answered Zorn.

CHAPTER 10

Room 205, Park Ave., New York City

"Where are we going with all of this," asked Annie Larkin as she sat in the small office opposite Michael Zorn. His desk was void of any papers normally found in a business office. No pictures or plaques hung on the walls, and the chairs were hand downs from government offices that had long ago upgraded. The office was not for public consumption. Larkin continued before Zorn could answer.

"I know that it might not be time for me to know the end game, but I think I have him where I want him. You saw the video I made. Why the continual updates regarding progress at the Freedom Tower. You can get that by walking by the place like a thousand tourists do every day. They stand and gawk, and no one bothers them. Why the details about access from the top, specifically to the core elevator shafts. He'll tell me anything because he likes to brag about how the tower is going up, but what is the connection?"

Zorn slid an envelope filled with twenties across the desk and gave a slight grin. "I believe you will get the picture eventually as the pieces come together. You do not have to know the reason why, but if the history books are ever privy to how what eventually happens came about, you will be a hero. Absurd as it sounds, sometimes there has to be a drastic act to get people to move to even more drastic actions.

"Take 9/11 for example. As horrible as it was, it brought this country together, and the actions in Iraq, although they are questioned today, set the tone that the United States will not tolerate any affront to its freedom. Saddam Hussein was purged from power and executed. Our war in Afghanistan to find Osama bin Laden took off with a lot of fanfare and support, but then, while our troops are busting their ass, Americans are only concerned about the economy. How much money they can make? There is very little flag waving anymore. Cars no longer have flags or patriotic bumper stickers. Those at home are lethargic when it comes to patriotism, and it is patriotism and love of country that has to be rejuvenated. I've said enough for now.

"On another note, who is this guy, Dick Gerardo?" Zorn asked. "I've run him in a few databases and was able to come up with a retired construction worker in Florida, who previously worked in New York years ago."

As part of the backstopping for his undercover part, the FBI came up with a Richard Gerardo from Tampa, Florida who was actually a retired construction worker. Unknown to the real Gerardo, this would be Gerosa's temporary identity. He wanted a same first name and a last name beginning with the same initial as his, and also an Italian name. Gerosa would also carry a social security card with Gerardo's number on it in his wallet.

"That's him," said Larkin. "He came back up here to do some work for a guy he used to work for years ago. Got Burke some side work, and is a good spender when it comes to dinner and booze. No flag waver either. But he's harmless. Made a pass at me a couple of times when Kieran was in the men's room or making a phone call, and I brushed it off, but hinted that it was not out of the question. Did it in case he could ever fit into the big picture. You never know. He's single and seems to have a good life."

Zorn thought for a moment. "Single? From what I got off the databases, he is married. He told you he was single?"

"Yeah, but what the hell, if he can be helpful in some way, I could probably get to him."

"Get any romantic ideas out of your head. When this is all over, Burke will be gone, and most likely Gerardo and you will be going to another part of the country."

"And where is Burke going?"

"Not for now, but it is in my plan and others to see that he is amply rewarded, and out of the country safely," responded Zorn. "How secure is your apartment?"

"What do you mean?" The question came out of nowhere, and Larkin looked puzzled.

"Does the landlord have access? Is there a good lock on your window near the fire escape?" Zorn leaned forward placing his elbows on the desk.

"He is supposed to, but I put another dead bolt lock on the door. As far as the window, it had double steel bars across it. They are bolted well into the wall, so I feel pretty secure when I am alone. Sometimes Burke stays the night, but not that often because he has to be at the site by 6:45, and that means leaving my place at 5:30 to get the bus to the subway and so forth. "

"I may want you to store something there for me until it is time for its use." Zorn did not wait for the obvious question, but looked at her with a slight smile. "Dynamite, several sticks of it, a couple of small suitcases full or perhaps suitcases full of C4."

Larkin showed no emotion as Zorn had expected. He had seen her in action in the past. She was cold. Her only reaction was mercenary.

"If I am going to be sitting on a powder keg, perhaps my stipend should go up."

"Your stipend is sufficient. Let me say that when this is over you won't have any money worries for the rest of your life, and can take a respectable job somewhere selling lingerie."

"I don't think so," was the response. "Is Kieran to know about this?"

"Of course, in time, and it is very simple. You tell him that you have a plan to put it to use, and you are receiving direction from very powerful people that think the way the both of you do, and want to send a message to the United States government. I'll leave it up to you if you want to use the term Muslim extremists. He has sympathies there from his past, and from what you have been telling me, and what I have seen, you have reached a point now where you can manipulate him into virtually doing whatever you want. Your mind control has been successful. How would he feel about putting his life in danger in furtherance of what you want?"

"I don't think that'll be a problem. You saw what he did with the gun. Right now, I am controlling his thinking, behavior and decision-making at least when it comes to his views of America. And he is ready to act out on my suggestions, once you tell me what you want him to do. Depending on the intensity, and the fallout of what he's directed to do, I might need a week to get him to comply, but I am sure it can be done."

Zorn leaned back in his chair, deep in thought. "When the time is right, and it will be shortly, we will have a general plan, but he will not get the specifics until the day before."

Larkin suddenly felt alone, and unlike her

previous capers for the CIA, there were too many unanswered questions with this one. Not that she cared as long as she got paid, but she also wanted to ensure her own safety.

"Listen Michael, I've done enough for the Agency to know that they have the full authority of at least the director, and in some situations, the president himself in anything they do. Is this the same?"

Zorn gave a forced laugh. "Of course. Don't you worry about the reason things are being done, and will be done. It all comes from the highest levels, and in the long run will be crucial to saving American lives, no matter what it looks like at the inception. Now get out of here, and go about your business but make sure you check in every day as things might change."

Larkin nodded and left. On her way to the elevator, she passed a middle-aged man in a business suit that emerged from one of the other offices. He paid no attention to her, as it was the unwritten rule of those who used the small offices on that floor to not ask questions of nor greet anyone coming to or going from any of the offices. Not even stare at them, as they were all part of a government approved operation.

Although there were several reasons for saying it, Zorn did not like the fact that Gerardo passed himself off as being single.

CHAPTER 11

Gerosa's Apartment

It was 6:30 am and Gerosa was dozing after a bad night of sleep. He had dinner the night before with a secretary from the office, and it was uneventful. He tried his best to get her back to his apartment contrary to Michaels' counsel that it was an undercover apartment and off limits to any office personnel or anyone else, but his efforts failed.

Heavy fog filled the air as he gazed out of his kitchen window while downing his first cup of coffee. His thoughts consumed where his latest caper was going, as they were during his restless night's sleep. An Irish construction worker, an office cleaner, a former CIA agent and what appeared to be a federal judge and an entrepreneur were all in some kind of bizarre conspiracy. But to do what. He was becoming impatient.

"Eddie here," was the response after the third

ring on Michaels' cell phone.

"Want to go for a ride or do you have to play construction worker today?"

"Why, do you need a lookout?" Michaels knew exactly what Gerosa had in mind.

"It's a good day to drive. No chopper will be going up there today, and I figure that we can be there within three hours. I'll be by your apartment in about half an hour."

Michaels hung up the phone and was trading the construction boots and trousers that he had just put on for black Levi's and running shoes.

Nancy Schaeffer, barely awake as she rolled to his side of the bed, saw the change of clothes. "What's going on Eddie? Why the change? You're supposed to be at the site today and hang around looking for suspicious people." She was being sarcastic.

"I've got to do something with Dick."

"You know, Eddie, ever since he came back to something that you won't discuss, you've spent a lot of time with him on what you say is something important. Don't I have a right to know? Aren't you supposed to be on your swan song? On the way out of the Bureau? We've been together for how long? And you can't even discuss what you are doing with me."

Michaels was sitting on the side of the bed as he tied his pair of black New Balance running shoes. "Something came up related to the site that I have to take care of. It will be over soon. Just bear with me on this."

"Sure Eddie," she said seething. "Another Goddamn windmill. Just like the old days. You and Dick. Starsky and Hutch. Why don't you marry him, you spend more time with him than with me ever since he came back to New York? You want me out of here tonight? Do you want to run with Dick to the bars and nightclubs again? If so, I'm gone. And to be honest, I don't know if I'll be back. I have a chance to do international flights and lay over in some nice places like Paris, Belgium, and some nice cities in Germany."

"No Nancy, that's not what I want, and you know it," Michaels answered.

"No, I don't know it and, frankly, you don't show it."

Michaels decided silence was best when she was in this mood. But she was never this vocal. She rolled over in the bed, turning away from him, so a kiss goodbye was out of the question. He heard her stifle a sob with her pillow as he closed the door. What the hell, I do owe her a little more or at least an explanation or am I just jealous thinking of her in the arms of a 747 captain while in some romantic city.

The ride to Wyndham in Gerosa's pickup truck was mostly spent reminiscing about previous cases that they had worked and the moments that were for one reason or another, never put into a report. They also speculated as to the roles of the principals of their latest case.

What do you make of it?" Michaels asked. "You've been with this guy and his girlfriend several times, and we know that she is contacting the Director of Homeland Security for New York State, a former CIA agent, who in turn is meeting with a federal judge and a businessman in the tech business."

Michaels was staring out the side window, trying to put the pieces together. "I'm hoping that our ride up here will answer some of the questions. Burke is not the smartest guy around, but is a hard worker and one of these guys who will probably go back to Ireland every year for a vacation. I checked to see if he was still associated with the IRA. Today, there is a spinoff known as the REAL IRA because they still want to bomb Northern Ireland establishments. In August of '98, there was the Omagh bombing in County Tyrone, which killed twenty-nine people and injured around 220. After the bombing, the RIRA went on a ceasefire, but surfaced again in 2000. And in March 2009, RIRA members claimed responsibility for killing two British soldiers during an attack on the Massereene Barracks. They were the first to be killed in Northern Ireland since 1997.

"I reached out to some Garda that I know in Ireland and even The Yard and, according to them, Burke left that scene several years ago. He either calmed down in his radical beliefs or went into a deep cover."

Gerosa interrupted. "I would guess the latter

because of his association with the radical Muslims in England. From what I see, he hasn't joined any groups here and is wrapped up in his work and with Larkin."

Michaels continued, "I thought about the Freedom Tower, and he is just one of several hundred workers down there that has the same access as all the others and that is to report to the foremen and go to work. He could have access to the construction managers' and superintendents' offices or shanties where the plans and the architects' drawings are kept, if he knew when they all go to the numerous meetings that they have every week.

"They have safety meetings, scheduling meetings, progress meetings and so on. But even if he does go into the offices or shanties undetected, there are volumes of blueprints, and he couldn't take them out without being noticed. So, he can't be passing info on to anyone. Besides, the television and newspaper updates give all that anyone would want to know."

"I hope this trip answers some of the questions," said Gerosa. He pulled into the parking lot of the Wyndham Country Club, where a few pickup trucks were parked, their occupants engaged in aerating the greens and replacing sand in the traps. His truck blended in as that of a supervisor of the company doing the work.

"We walk from here," said Michaels, "It is only about a half mile." Gerosa slung his backpack over his shoulder, and they walked to the main road. Fifteen minutes later they went into the brush on the side of the road to cover any tracks they might make and made their way to a vantage point where they could determine if there were any occupants of the cabin.

"Eddie, I'm retired, but you're still on the job, so there is no need for you to be privy to any of this stuff. Wait here and hit your speed dial on the cell if anyone shows up."

"10-4," said Michaels as Gerosa lowered his pack and pulled out a set of keys, a flashlight, a small electronic device, and a couple of clean rags, which he stuffed in the pocket of his light windbreaker. Gerosa easily entered the front door with the keys that he made during his last visit and again paused, checking the room for any new motion detector alarms. There was none. The room was unchanged with the exception of some new magazines. He made his way to the coffee table, squatted, and without looking searched the underside with the palm of his right hand. "Ah yes," he whispered as his hand touched the familiar object, and he gently pried it away from the double-sided tape. He placed it on the table and removed a small electronic device from his pocket. Next, he connected both, turned them on, pressed a few switches and waited for whatever was on the recorder to be downloaded to his device. When the transfer was complete, he checked and saw that he had a recording on his device, after which he deleted what was on the recorder and replaced the batteries with two new ones. He placed it back under the coffee table.

Gerosa and Michaels made their way back to the truck in silence. A little game Gerosa played with Michaels. Wanted him to ask before he volunteered something.

"Okay, you smug son of a bitch, what do you have?" said Michaels as they pulled out of the parking lot.

"I got something because the recorder took a while to download. Let's see." He removed the device from his pocket and activated the play switch. Much of the initial talk was between Kirkland and Whitaker and was about world events. Enter Zorn and the conversation shifted and got right to the business of what they were planning, but they were not specific.

"I can't believe what I am hearing," said Gerosa, "Sounds like Zorn's playing a video where Larkin's got Burke into playing Russian roulette, but with a dummy round.

"He doesn't know that and like an obedient puppy he does what she says. Un fuckin' believable. What does she have over him? And what the hell does the mention of suggestive behavior have to do with this? Do they get their rocks off watching a video of someone jerking another one around with a fake Russian roulette game?"

Gerosa thought for a moment. "It can't be

sex. There is no shortage of women to make that guy chance a bullet in the head to go to bed with her. I remember taking a few hours of psychology at the Bureau school before I went on my first undercover assignment and during one of them, some renowned psychologist with all kinds of degrees, told us that we would basically run into two types when we went undercover. First, the sick bastards in charge of the criminal group, the leaders. They have their own agenda and feed off their underlings. It is the underlings who can be moved in one direction or the other because it is continually drilled into their heads that they have to do what the bosses want because of undying loyalty. It is a form of continuous suggestions as to what they should be doing and, being weak of character, they go along. I think that is what we have here. But to what end?

"The judge and our entrepreneur seem to be losing patience about something that is supposed to come down the pike," continued Gerosa. "I think I'll try and get a bit closer to Larkin. She's not bad looking and maybe she won't be able to resist my charm." Gerosa was grinning as the truck rolled down the New York Thruway.

Michaels glanced at the passing scenery and looked briefly at Gerosa. "Sure, that's just what we need. This whole thing comes together, and it surfaces that you were banging one of the defendants. How would that look?"

"I don't think this is a case that will ever

come to trial," Gerosa said. "What we've learned so far, no one in government would want in the papers. Besides, if it ever came out how we got the information, we could be planting vegetables in Otisville with the white-collar prisoners. On second thought, being ex feds, they'd probably put us with the worst, so they would beat the shit out of us."

"Dick, don't even think about her. I'm serious."

"Alright, I'll just do a little flirting to see if I can get her away from Burke and pick her brain."

"One more thing," said Michaels, "What are you going to do with the evidence you have obtained? Illegally." Michaels emphasized the word illegally.

"Don't know what you are talking about, Eddie." Gerosa winked. "There is no evidence. Only leads for us to work on. If everything comes to a successful conclusion, we can be creative and come up with the path that got us there. No one will give a shit if we prevent something bad from happening."

"I hope you're right, Dick. I'm catching some shit at home. Don't know how much longer Nancy's going to wait for me to make our relationship legit. First it was companionship, now it's for real. Once she knew you were in town, she knew something big was up and keeps peppering me with questions."

"I supposed she's pissed because she thinks we are out drinking and chasing women."

"No, she trusts me. Just wants more of my time and to settle down, or she may pull the plug on our relationship. Just today she talked about going on international routes. Don't know how I would handle that."

"Can't blame her. She's there for you and wants little in return except maybe marriage."

"That's a lot Dick. Done that dance before and look what happened. Thank God my ex had a decent job, or a piece of my pension would be gone."

"Ouch! As they say, take the house, the car, the boat, the dog, and anything else you want, but leave me my pension. The mantra of agents entering into divorce."

"You got that right," said Michaels.

"The way I see it, we have about a month or so," Gerosa said, "My guess is that something is planned for around 9/11 to send a message. Want me to come over and put on my Italian charm, so she knows we are doing something important, and it will end soon?"

"Dick, how long has she known you? She knows you are full of shit."

CHAPTER 12

Wyndham hunting lodge

Kirkland and Whitaker sipped coffee and were visibly annoyed as Zorn came through the door. They earlier consented to an emergency meeting on a weekend when they would normally not be at the lodge.

"I hope you realize what an inconvenience this is in addition to the security lapse if someone should question why we are up here two weekends in a row." Kirkland was visibly annoyed.

"It is important, so let me get to the point right away," said Zorn.

Whitaker exhaled and leaned back on the couch. "This better be good because as I told you, there is a lot of money at stake here."

Zorn stood and motioned to Whitaker and Kirkland to go outside with him, where they sat at an old picnic table several yards from the cabin. "I don't want to seem paranoid, but when was the last time that you had the cabin swept for any listening devices? An old CIA spook always thinks of these things, so just indulge me having to further discuss what we have to do out here. I'm not suspicious, only cautious, and when you hear what I have to say, you will know why."

Kirkland and Whitaker looked at each other, both a little annoyed. "Continue." ordered Kirkland. "But you are being a little paranoid."

"Just overly cautious. As you know, I have been monitoring all the information and pictures that Burke has been giving to Larkin, and we knew from the inception that the bomb wall surrounding the building up to the 20th floor would preclude any type of vehicle bomb from doing any damage. What we wanted to do is drop a large amount of explosives down the elevator shaft, programmed so that every five floors an altimeter would activate a blasting cap and then the explosives. There would first be an explosion and then an implosion and all the perimeter security would be negated, and the inner structure of the building would come down. Explosives were to be stored at Larkin's apartment, brought to the site piecemeal by Burke and locked up in one of the many gang boxes used by the laborers. He would have the only key to the lock. This would take about than five days, so no one would be suspicious."

"How does this all get inside the building," asked Kirkland.

"Burke could take a good amount in his

backpack and cooler that many of the workers bring into the site every day. Nothing is searched. At the designated time, Burke would be told to dump the explosives down one of the elevator shafts. He would not know about the altimeter activated blasting caps, which I can activate via my cell phone right before Burke dumps the explosives. Larkin would lead him to believe that the explosives are activated by the blasting caps ten minutes after they hit the bottom. We would tell him that a helicopter would come by and drop a line to him from the roof, and he would get away with a new ID before the explosion, etcetera, and go back to Ireland. Of course, this part would not happen, and Burke would end up like the other workers. No one would suspect him, and no one would know how the explosion occurred. Hopefully, the rubble would destroy Burke and any evidence."

"So, what's the problem?" asked Whitaker.

It bothered Kirkland that there now was a glitch. "Things have to move faster."

Zorn was hoping his new plan would sit well with the two powerful men sitting across from him. They were his ticket to success.

"As you know, I have been getting a steady flow of information and pictures from Larkin who gets them from Burke. I started thinking about the density and the psi of the concrete floors and walls, and the steel structure inside the concrete. I did some math and had an engineer take a look at the specs. His professional opinion is that no matter how many explosives were blown up on any given floor, or in this case, every five floors where the elevator shaft opens to the floor, the damage will only be minor and affect only the particular floor of the explosion. Nothing will come down. Shit, the core of the building is constructed so a 747 could come in from any side, and it would do some damage, but bounce off or crash into one floor without any additional damage. So, we have to scrap any plan involving explosives. It would take our guy a month to bring in enough to do any damage and he would probably get caught along the way. If he didn't get caught, there is still no place he could store that amount of dynamite." Zorn paused to get a reaction. "And we really don't know what the end result would be."

"So, all of this has been a waste of time. Why the fuck didn't you think of this before," asked Whitaker, visibly agitated.

"Wait." Kirkland said as he excused himself and went back into the cabin, returning with a bottle of scotch and two rocks glasses. His face was flushed, and he poured a few ounces into one glass and left the other on the table. "Do you have a backup plan now that this has gone down the shitter?"

"Yes," answered Zorn. "Sarin. It is a colorless, odorless gas, and is man made. Exposure can cause convulsions, paralysis, and loss of consciousness and can cause death by respiratory failure. The good part is that I have the connections to get some that is already made. It has been used successfully in the past in small incidents. When the Japanese terrorists let some loose in a subway in Tokyo, 12 people were killed. It is anathema to all peace-loving nations, particularly the United States, and is associated with terrorism. Even without proof, Al-Qaeda will be blamed."

"How much is needed and when can you get this?" asked Whitaker as he grabbed the other glass, poured himself some scotch and sounded disgusted by the change in plans.

Zorn anticipated this question and had the answer. "Do you think that the U S has been sitting around complaining about the use of sarin in Syria and doing nothing? I happen to know that the Agency has been secretly buying large amounts of liquid sarin from Syria. They pay dearly for it, but that is no problem with a budget that is unlimited and unaccounted for. A behind the scenes deal has been made that we buy up all the sarin that they have Therefore it will not be used against the rebels. The flaw is that the people that the Agency are dealing with are selling it claiming that it is coming from numerous stockpiles, whereas in reality, they are producing it as fast as we are buying it."

"So, what is the U.S., or I should say we, doing with it?" asked Kirkland as he took a sip of his scotch.

"It's being destroyed. But naturally the Agency can't say it is sarin, and it is disposed of somewhere in the west along with radioactive material that is also disposed of there. A government contractor picks it up at a storage point along with radioactive waste and transports it to the disposal site once a month. It is in liquid form and is contained in sealed metal tubes, four of which are sealed in 50-gallon drums, the way radioactive waste is disposed of. The drums are sealed in wooden crates, the crates are unloaded, and the drums dumped at the disposal site in a deep hole and covered with soil immediately just like the radioactive waste. It is a careful packing process because the liquid turns to gas if it is exposed to the atmosphere and quickly spreads into the environment, harming and usually killing anyone with whom it has contact. Can you imagine the outcry if this ever happened?"

"So how do you get hold of it and how do we use it?" asked Kirkland. This piqued Whitaker's interest as he moved forward on the bench.

Zorn continued, "Let's take this one step at a time. First of all, the sarin is not disposed of regularly with the waste because, although we buy what we can, it is not always plentiful. When the Agency gets it, it is packaged and mixed in with the radioactive waste. The key is knowing when it is being shipped and what crates inside the truck contain the sarin.

"Go on," said Kirkland, pouring himself

another scotch and waving the bottle towards Whitaker, who accepted his offer and poured a double.

"I checked out the contractor who moves the radioactive waste. It wasn't easy because this thing is completely under wraps, more so with the sarin, and I had to go to extremes to get the info I am about to tell you. The contractor, B & G Hauling usually moves garbage over the road from transfer stations to landfills on tractor-trailers. The government put out a bid request to move what they referred to as radioactive waste from nuclear power stations to a landfill somewhere in the Midwest approved by the EPA. B & G won the contract. As far as they know, they are hauling sealed wooden crates in which there are sealed drums of radioactive waste, and the movement has been approved by every government agency that has a concern. Of course, the company couldn't give a shit less what they are hauling as long as they make money."

"How do we know which of the crates contains the sarin?' asked Kirkland, again becoming impatient.

"Good question. Two drums are packed in one crate, and there are usually four crates on a truck. They don't move them in large quantities for fear of the outrage should there be an accident in some small town en route. Each crate has a number on it, and the crate containing the sarin starts with 666, ironically the devil's number.

Someone has a sick sense of humor.

"On one of B & G's trips, when I knew the 666 crates were being transported, I had the trailer followed and found that the driver stops at a small motel that caters to truck drivers," Zorn said.

"Stop right there," Whitaker interrupted. "Who the hell is doing all this? The surveillance and whatever the hell else you have them doing. How much do they know about what is going on?"

Zorn anticipated this question. "Ed, be assured that they have no knowledge of the end game or who you or the judge are. I deal with them personally. They don't even know me by my right name. They think that they are dealing with someone who is currently with the Agency and what they are doing has the Agency behind them. If things turn to shit, and they try to give me up, no one would be able to find me. I deal with them by burner phone, and my alias has no connection with the Agency."

"Who are they and where did they come from?" asked Kirkland, not quite confident in Zorn's answer.

"They are a bunch of black ops guys who were contractors in Afghanistan. Did all kinds of shit that we wouldn't do in areas where we wouldn't go. When they got back here, they put together a security and investigation company and do things that an ordinary PI company wouldn't do. They don't ask questions because they make good money, untraceable money, that I get from the Agency, and they believe they are still serving their country."

Kirkland and Whitaker looked at each other and nodded. "Go on," said Kirkland.

"As I mentioned," Continued Zorn, "the driver carrying what we want regularly stops at a low rate motel where he can sleep in a bed rather than in his cab. Big parking area in the back where trucks come and go all night. My guys got into the trailer and took pictures of the crates containing the sarin. They have no idea what is in them, and they know better than to ask."

"What else do they do?" asked Whitaker as he sipped from his glass of scotch.

"They know the crating, which is supposed to contain drums of radioactive waste and marked with 666. They have duplicated these two crates and loaded them up with similar drums filled with water. They don't know what is in the original crates and drums and don't give a damn. Good soldiers – just do as they're ordered and ask no questions.

"Within the next week, when I know the sarin is being moved, they will follow the truck and while the driver sleeps, they are going to remove the sarin from the truck and replace it with crates containing the water filled drums.

"They have the forklift and a similar truck to do this quickly and efficiently. They will drop the crates in an area that I designate, and I will go there, retrieve them and take them to a self-storage unit I rented in Yonkers."

"What next?" asked Whitaker. Zorn now had their undivided attention and loved every minute of it.

"At this point, their job is done. All they know is that for whatever reason, they are taking two crates containing drums of radioactive waste off a truck and dropping them at a place I will designate. After that, they are done. They know nothing more.

"Once in the storage unit, I have another operative, a former mechanic who was surveyed out of the Air Force because of his right-wing views and is always looking for a buck. He has been used by the Agency as a contractor, mostly overseas in putting together explosives, the type and size of which we disclaim to have. He is an accomplished welder, and again, doesn't ask questions. He has been told that I have a special job for him to put explosives in acetylene tanks to be sold to terrorist groups. Once they turn the tanks on to weld something, it goes boom and we win again.

"He will take the sarin canisters, which are about three feet high and six inches in diameter, and insert them into empty acetylene tanks used for the torches that some of the trades regularly use at the site. He already went to a scrapyard and got several outdated and drained tanks and cut the bottoms off where the canisters of sarin can be inserted. He has no clue about the sarin and believes that all that is going into the tanks are explosives to kill terrorists. He will then weld the bottom back on after packing the free space with C4 and leave an opening at the removable cap on top where he will insert more C4 and a blasting cap and a miniature digital altimeter with an on-off switch. He will be told that the altimeter is nothing more than a radio-controlled device that could set off the blasting cap at our control should the tank not go off or the terrorists get suspicious.

"I already figured the amount of explosives that will blow the tank open and blow up the canister, dispersing the sarin all over the place. The liquid will quickly evaporate into the air and people won't know what hit them. The altimeter, once activated, will cause the tanks to blow every three floors. I figure Burke can only get a few over the edge before he begins to feel the effects as some of the sarin rises from the elevator shaft. Until that point all that he will hear are the explosions and figure that it is only dynamite."

Whitaker interrupted. "You left something out. There is a big gap from the storage area to the site where Burke dumps them down the shaft."

Zorn grinned. "I already have it set up that once the tanks are ready, Larkin will accompany Burke who will be sent to the storage area on a Sunday morning and load four of the tanks into a small truck. I'll see if he can borrow one from the construction companies where he now does some weekend work. That will make it a legitimate delivery and the guards at the gate won't be suspicious because they all know Burke and he has all the right passes. Burke puts them on a handcart two at a time and goes up the hoist to wherever the top happens to be at the time. Probably the 70th floor. Right before this, he takes a gang box storage unit from one of the other trades on a lower floor, spray paints over the company name, locks it and puts it near his shanty close to the top. A few trips will do it, and he has eight tanks ready to go. On Wednesday, there is scheduled the regular safety meeting and all of the laborers and ironworkers have to meet on the sixth floor for the meeting, so Burke will be alone. The best part is that if everything goes as planned, this will happen on 9/12. One day after 9/11. On 9/11 and the days before, there will be a load of security there, but after the 11th, everyone will feel secure.

"I will have all the tanks numbered to correspond to when the altimeter sets them off; number 1 being the first to go and to detonate at street level. The next at 30 feet and so forth."

Whitaker turned to Kirkland. "Know what I like about it? It has foreign terrorist written all over it. With explosives, there would be the liberals screaming that it was a right-wing nut job or a homegrown terrorist. This way there is no doubt that it came from Al-Qaeda and when Mike has some fake intelligence surface from overseas that the plan came from some cells in Afghanistan, the withdrawal that is planned will cease and there will be a full out war effort."

Kirkland walked around the picnic table, his mind weighing the advantages against the disadvantages of the new plan. "I will go along with it, but if something goes wrong, there is no way it can come back to us, meaning Ed and me. You better have a plan to abort if things start to go wrong. Do I make myself clear?"

"Perfectly," said Zorn without hesitation. If anything went really bad, his plans were already made. He would leave the country under a new identity and spend out his days in Europe and give a shit less about the two pompous individuals in front of him.

"If we are done, let's get back inside," said Whitaker as he and Kirkland went towards the cabin and Zorn went to his SUV.

CHAPTER 13

Roberto's restaurant, Yonkers, NY

"So you're getting to like my kind of food?" Gerosa sat across the table from Larkin and Burke. This was their second time at Roberto's, an upscale Italian restaurant in Yonkers, as part of what became a weekly ritual for dinner and drinks. Neither Larkin nor Burke cared as long as Gerosa picked up the tab, which he always did. The conversation to this point had always been social, discussing work or current events, frequently disparaging the current administration in Washington. This evening, Gerosa decided to probe a little deeper.

"So Annie, where do you work? I know what you do, but how are the people you work for? Do they pay well? Reason I'm asking is that maybe I can get you an office job where I am."

"I've got several small office buildings downtown that I clean. Was put in touch with them through a friend. By hiring me directly, they save the extra fees of an agency." Experience taught her to always be vague when asked anything about her line of work. She stared at Gerosa as if waiting for the next question. There was none.

They had just finished the main course, and were waiting to order dessert and coffee when Burke fidgeted in his chair. "I think I need a smoke. Goin' outside. Order me a Jameson's straight up when the waiter comes back. Annie, you comin' with me?"

She could have used a smoke, but decided a one-on-one with Gerosa was more important. Maybe she could get some additional information for Zorn.

"No, I'll wait." As soon as Burke left, she moved her foot against Gerosa's under the table, and smiled at him. "So where exactly do you live, Mr. Gerardo?" she asked with a sly smile, using the term Mr. as opposed to Dick, which she usually called him.

Gerosa was taken back. *What the hell is going on here? I'm supposed to be doing the flirting,* thought Gerosa. He decided to play along.

"I'm in an apartment in Pelham Bay. Quiet street, nice neighbors. I ought to have you and Kieran over some time. I'm a pretty good cook."

"Do you have a wife or girlfriend?"

"Neither. Left them both in Florida. If you want to know if I am still married, the answer is no." Gerosa had to think if the identity he assumed was someone who was married.

"Maybe I'd like to stop by alone sometime. Kieran is nice, and although we spend most of our time together at my place, it is the same thing every day; work, drink, and get ready for the next day."

"Just let me know a day in advance," said Gerosa as Burke returned to the table.

When they finished their after-dinner drinks, coffee and dessert, Gerosa drove them back to Katonah Ave., and dropped them off at Larkin's apartment. Inside, Larkin brought Burke into the kitchen.

"Sit down. I have something important to tell you." Burke obediently pulled up a chair, a little groggy from the last Jameson.

"I need you to help me with something." Larkin was dead serious, and knew that she had Burke at the point where he would do anything that she asked, particularly if it was anti-establishment. She was positive of this after the test with the revolver. She leaned towards him and smiled.

"I am going to be storing something in a nearby self-storage place and at the right time you will be taking it down to the site where you will use it to become a hero, and send a message to all those capitalists who are paying you a lousy thirty dollars an hour."

"What are you talking about?"

She leaned across the table and whispered. "Dynamite." Zorn did not tell her that there was a change from dynamite to sarin gas for fear she or Burke might back out. Dynamite was Burke's thing, and he would probably be comfortable with it.

"Fuckin' dynamite. I'm used to playing around with that from me previous life. And what might I ask are you going to be doing with the dynamite?" She now had Burke's attention.

"It's not me, it is us. I will be getting the dynamite from a source that I have. Unfortunately, I cannot give you all the details now, but you will make a pickup in a rented storage space at a location in Yonkers. The explosives will be there secreted in empty acetylene tanks.

"You will bring them to the Freedom Tower on a Sunday, and store them in a gang box. Shortly thereafter, at my or my boss's command, you will dump them down one of the elevator shafts. They have a ten-minute timer, which will give you time to be lifted off the top in a helicopter."

Larkin waited for a reaction knowing full well that a helicopter couldn't get within a hundred yards of the building without attracting law enforcement attention, and would be shot down if it disobeyed directives. The question was would Burke believe this cockamamie scenario. She believed that she still had mind control over him, and exercised it every night in one form or another.

"Jesus fuckin' Christ," said Burke, "this makes the IRA look like amateurs. And where might I go in the whirlybird?"

"Listen Kieran, when the dynamite goes off, do you think anyone is going to give a shit about your helicopter? Cops, fireman, security people will all be rushing to the scene, and the sky will be full of news helicopters. No one will notice that you are even there. The chopper will take you to Westchester County Airport where you will be given a new identity, and in short time, be on a plane for Fort Lauderdale. From there you will catch a flight to Shannon airport, and be met with one of our operatives who will give you lodging and a briefcase full of money. From then on, it is up to you."

"But will they know it was me? I might want to get some recognition as the man who took down the symbol of oppression. Might make me look good in some circles."

Larkin couldn't believe this stupid question, although she recognized that he was in for the whole scenario.

"Kieran, you have to understand that with your present identity, you will be hunted down by every agency in the free world. This way, you have your new identity, but when they figure out it was you who did it, your name will go down in history. A terrorist to some and a hero to others."

Burke thought for a moment. "You make

sense, Annie. I'll go with the program. Maybe you can join me, and as they say, live happily ever after."

Annie smiled. "Of course, we can work that out. I enjoy being with you Kieran, and this life here is boring."

No Goddamn way is that ever going to happen, she thought.

CHAPTER 14

Truck stop Route 70 Springfield, Illinois

Joe Sullivan had been with B & G Hauling for over 25 years, and was one of their few over-the-road drivers who management would trust with handling a cargo of radioactive waste. His run from Pennsylvania to the Yucca Mountains in southern Nevada began a year ago, and was always uneventful. He expected the same for this trip. He liked the twenty-two-foot straight truck that was usually half full because of the nature of the cargo, rather than a tractor-trailer loaded with garbage going to a landfill, which he previously drove.

His current cargo, sixteen 50-gallon metal drums, all purportedly filled with waste, were welded closed, and packed two each in a heavy wooden crate and put on a pallet. Sullivan carted eight such pallets in his straight truck. This day, two of the drums contained four cylinders of sarin each, and were filled with water. He left Pennsylvania earlier in the day, and the

Department of Transportation required a stop, so he could not drive through, which he would have preferred.

"Your room is ready, Joe" the desk clerk and part owner of the motel said as Sullivan walked up to the small receptionist desk.

"How was the trip?" a question he always asked out of force of habit. Sullivan always gave the same answer. "Uneventful."

Sullivan regularly frequented the small truck stop motel off US 70 in Springfield. His needs amounted to a few hours sleep and a hot shower, and the motel served this purpose, although his room lacked the amenities found at a Marriott and emitted a mixture of unfamiliar odors. A square wooden structure with two floors, Sullivan always took a room in the rear from where he could see his truck. The motel rooms were for eight-hour periods and turned over quickly as some drivers preferred driving at night to make better time.

"And here is your high octane diesel," the desk clerk said, pulling a small brown bag out from under the counter. He passed the half pint of whiskey to Sullivan along with the room key. Sullivan had already parked his truck in the back lot, checked the locks, and did a walk around to check the tires, and for any oil leaks. "Thank you, Henry. What would I do without you?"

There wasn't a liquor store within miles, so over the months the desk clerk made a habit of giving Sullivan a half pint of Seagram's whenever he checked in. A $5.00 tip over the price showed Sullivan's appreciation. He gave a wave as he went off to his back room, and raised the dirty shade so he could take a look at his truck. The lot was well lit, and trucks came and went up to midnight. After that, there was only occasional movement. He checked the bed to decide if he would sleep on top or under the sheets if they were clean, and not a leftover from a short stay by a couple of cheaters. He went through his ritual of smelling the pillowcase and checking the sheets for stains. No perfume, no stains. The sheets would do.

Sullivan admired the bottle of Seagram's, unscrewed the cap, and took a long swig. He relished the warmth rising in his throat, and checked his watch. Not too late to call his wife. After the perfunctory telephone call ending with "I love you," Sullivan took another swig, stripped down, and took a long-awaited hot shower.

The occupant of a late model Chevy Tahoe parked at the end of the lot in view of Sullivan's room spoke into a two-way encrypted radio. "Lights out. Another hour and it's showtime."

"Roger that" came the response.

The three other former military and special ops people now working as a little-known consulting firm kept busy with contracts from individuals who were usually three removed from the actual source, which most times was some little known government agency, a spinoff of NSA, CIA, or Army Intel. No questions were ever asked, and they knew if anything went wrong, they were on their own. They risked this for the generous compensation they received.

"Let's do it." The leader of the group ordered the person in a rented Ryder straight truck identical to Sullivan's that was parked nearby. The night was ideal for their task; overcast with a threat of a storm. Rain would serve as a good cover, and a drizzle just started.

Inside the motel, Sullivan poured the remains of the whiskey into a water glass, and put it on the table next to his bed. There was no television in this budget truck stop, so Sullivan lay back against the headboard, thought for a few moments, and downed what was left of the Seagram's. He slid down in the bed, dozing off thinking of his next vacation in the Catskills.

There was silence as one of the team cut the back lock, and rolled up the door of Sullivan's truck as another backed the rental truck against it. Pallets containing the sarin identified by the number 666 were removed, and replaced with similar crates containing 50-gallon drums of water. At the end of the transfer, the sky opened, and a torrential rain began.

"Move it," commanded the leader as the small forklift operator put the last sarin pallet into place while another strapped them down inside the truck. A deafening thunderbolt hit nearby causing a slight jolt of electricity shoot through the wet pavement. One of the men blessed himself while another laughed.

The sound awoke Sullivan. He rose from his bed and rushed to the window to check his truck. Seeing the second truck backed up to it, he dressed quickly. Running through the rain, squinting to keep it from blurring his vision.

"What the hell is going on here?" He slowed as he approached the one standing near the rear of the truck. Sullivan saw the black clothing and ski mask. He stopped abruptly within ten feet of the cab.

The downpour and silencer dulled the one high-powered shot from a .32 caliber Glock fired by the person that Sullivan was approaching. The round pierced Sullivan's chest and exited his back, and he barely hit the ground when a second individual came from behind the cab and dragged him to the rear of the truck.

The person in charge got out of the Tahoe and barked orders as he pointed to the others after seeing that Sullivan was dead.

"You, go to his room and get the keys to the truck and clean it out. Don't let anyone see you. Try the window if you can't bypass the front desk."

He checked Sullivan's body, and rolled it over to see if the bullet pierced his chest without hitting bone and exited the back. It had, and he smiled. He knew the pouring rain would wash away any traces of blood.

"You and you," he directed two of the others, "Put him in the passenger seat, and do it quickly before he gets too drenched," as he pointed at Sullivan's lifeless body. "When we get the keys, one of you will drive and follow me." The two pallets were locked down in the second truck. One of the men drove it into the shadows, waiting for the others.

The one returning with the keys had Sullivan's shaving kit. He smiled and showed the empty whiskey bottle to the leader.

"Could this fit in with your plan?" The leader smiled. "Perfect. When they find him in the truck, they will think he got drunk, couldn't sleep, and moved on to his destination. I'll lead, and when we get to the ravine near the small bridge about five miles from here in the direction he would have been going, slide him over to the driver's seat, and point the truck towards the ravine. Goose the gas and get the hell away from it." The driver nodded, and within a few minutes the Tahoe led the two trucks out of the lot.

The team briefly watched the truck and its contents break apart as it tumbled onto the rocks below.

"Done," said the leader. "Now let's get the hell out of here." He made his call to Zorn, telling him that he had the goods, but did not mention what they did with Sullivan and the truck. *Let him think what he wants. My report is that it went smoothly.*

What the driver did after we left is not my concern.

CHAPTER 15

New York FBI office, 26 Federal Plaza

In addition to the sign-in sheet, each attendee had to pass through a TSA advanced technology imaging scanner. It was similar to the ones used at airports to screen passengers for metallic and nonmetallic threats, including weapons and explosives, which could be concealed under clothing. In this case, it was also looking for, and was keyed to pick up any hidden recording device or a cell phone, unlike the one in the lobby that just checked Michael Zorn for guns or knives.

Zorn religiously attended the weekly security briefings held in the conference room at the FBI office. It was the time and place to schmooze the other so called security experts in attendance, and pick up tidbits of what was happening in the world of secrecy; tidbits that could enhance or alter the plan that he had already set in motion.

As Zorn entered the conference room, Eddie Michaels stood nearby and observed the attendees sign-in and present identification before they entered the room, although most were known among the group. On a nearby table sat a pigeonholed cabinet where attendees were directed to place their cell phones. Briefcases were placed in a line under the table.

"Good morning, Mr. Zorn" said the FBI secretary as she looked at his identification. "By the way," she continued, "Are you related to the Zorns in Bridgeport?" Zorn stopped, partially because he wanted to be polite and answer her question, and partially because she was very attractive. Michaels chose her for that reason.

No, I'm not," he responded.

"Just thought I'd ask," the secretary said. "I used to know a Mary Zorn who lives there." She had already researched a Zorn family in Bridgeport, CT, where her daughter, Mary, was in college.

Michaels was not privy to attend these meetings, but was off to the side to covertly take a picture of Zorn, which he did, the secretary giving him the opportunity to take several shots with the camera concealed in a briefcase. He looked at her after Zorn went into the meeting room and mouthed "Thank you."

A former rear admiral, now the deputy director of the CIA, gave the briefings shortly after flying to New York on the shuttle from Washington, DC. A short, stocky man in an ill-fitting suit, common among those that recently made the transition from military to civilian, he approached the small podium and silenced the meaningless banter that had been going on among the attendees. He was all business, and saw no need for coffee and doughnuts, the usual snacks for such meetings.

"Gentlemen," he started as his eyes perused the room to signify that he was directly speaking to each attendee personally.

"The first order of business is that I received a briefing before I left this morning from the director of my agency, and after debating whether it should be a matter for discussion at this and future meetings, we decided that it was of such importance that it should at least be mentioned.

"Before I start, I want to reinforce my statements regarding the security of these meetings, and say that nothing that is discussed here goes beyond here unless there is an imminent threat to personnel or property, and then, with my approval. This is presently not the case. It is something I want you to file in the back of your heads, and be alert for within any ongoing investigations that your respective agencies might be conducting, no matter how crazy it might sound. That includes informant information and anonymous letters or telephone calls."

The deputy director paused and scanned the room. "The key word here is sarin. Or poison gas or chemical weapons or weapons of mass destruction. Eight canisters of sarin gas were taken from a truck carrying them for disposal. Where they came from or where they were going is irrelevant. Suffice to say that the truck driver had an accident, and what was supposed to be different cargo sealed in 50-gallon drums was actually the sarin gas, and it disappeared and was substituted with drums of water. During the accident investigation and the autopsy of the driver, a sharp medical examiner saw that the cause of death was not the crash, but a bullet through his heart, even though the initial finding was that the driver had been drinking and ran off the road.

"No bullet was found, so it is presumed that he was shot, and his body driven into a ravine where his truck and body were found. We wouldn't have learned of the switch of the drums in which the sarin was contained had a couple of the drums not split open when the truck came apart as it tumbled down, and spilled out plain water. So, this is a serious matter, and something that cannot, I stress cannot, get out to the media. There would be chaos if it did. Need I say more?"

"Where did this accident happen?" asked one of the attendees.

"In the Midwest. That's all I can say at this time, but we believe that whoever did this is part of a national network, and could be the beginning of a terrorist operation."

The room was silent. Zorn shifted in his seat. He silently cursed the people who had the engagement to get the sarin. If the goddamn drums didn't break open, there would have been no issue. They would have been removed and brought to the disposal site without further inquiry. Now it was out that the sarin was gone, and there was a homicide involved. He sat through the rest of the presentation and solicitation of the attendees for security items of interest. He had nothing to say and was oblivious to what was being said, concentrating on what his next move would be. There was no way, he thought, that Kirkland or Whitaker could ever learn that his operation fucked up.

Zorn had just left the FBI building. After considering asking the deputy director for more details about the sarin investigation, he decided to pass so as not to highlight his interest. He was hoping that one of the other attendees would drill down on the information, but no one did.

Zorn recently bought a thirty-day disposable phone and was irate as he spoke. His calls to Larkin were basically innocuous. They could be explained, but this phone was necessary for other calls, which he could not explain. The anonymity served his purpose.

"What the fuck went on?" Zorn gave no hello or polite greeting.

The former Navy SEAL knew what Zorn was talking about. "Mike, we never thought the drums would break open and that everything would go as planned. No need to tell you when there wasn't going to be a problem."

"Well guess what.   There is a big problem when I hear about it at a briefing."

"How much do they know?"

"Only that there is something very important missing. So now the FBI will be investigating the shit out of it. You better have covered your tracks well."

"What the hell are you talking about? What was in the containers that make it so important?"

"Nothing that you need to know about. Just let me know if any law enforcement or Homeland Security agency is making inquiries about you or anyone in your team. Where are the drums now, and when can I meet you and put them on my truck?" Zorn did not hide his irritability.

"They are stored in a secure location, believe me, and based on the interest in this cargo, the sooner I get rid of them and get paid, the happier I will be."

Zorn paused for a moment. "I will call you within the next two days and give you a location where I can meet with you and pick up the cargo. It will be in broad daylight in an industrial area, so no one will be suspicious. As soon as that is done, destroy that phone you have. If necessary, I know how to contact you."

Zorn saw no need to continue and hung up. He also saw no reason to derail his plan, and it could be pulled off without Kirkland and Whitaker's knowledge of the current events.

Eddie Michaels watched Zorn make his phone call from the lobby at 26 Federal Plaza and was hoping that it would come up on the records of Zorn's phone that they were monitoring, but doubted that it would. From what he knew about Zorn, he was a professional, and doubted that he would leave himself open with a sinister call from his personal phone. Zorn moved up the street to the subway station, and Michaels saw no reason to attempt to follow him. He returned to the elevator bank, took one to the twenty-second floor, flashed his ID to the security clerk, and proceeded directly to Dean's office. Susan, his secretary, gave him a look of disdain as he bypassed her, peeked in and said "Hi" to her before entering when he saw that there were no visitors.

"Did you know that your goddamn friend, and our premier undercover, is hitting on my secretary?" Dean was kidding because he knew Gerosa well.

"What do you expect, Rick? He's single, away from his current stable in Florida, and a man has his needs," said Michaels with a smile.

"How did you find out because I already knew? He asked me if she was still single and unattached."

"Don't you know caller ID comes up on my phone as well as hers when a call comes in. Just because I sit behind this desk, I still have some investigative skills. Now what do you want except to tell me you need more time to continue to pursue some harebrained case."

"Rick, you know that I have a nose for these things, and I believe that there is something important going on here because of the characters involved. Do you know what was discussed at the security briefing today?"

"No, I'm not privy to that info. All I know is that right now, we are not a priority for the surveillance squad, and from what you said this Larkin woman has no unusual contacts except Zorn. This probably is some kind of CIA operation that we are about to fuck up by having Gerosa interfere with it. Zorn seems to be doing nothing out of the ordinary, except for his meetings at the cabin. They could be completely harmless. The only thing that puzzles me is the recording that we have of some sort of video of what appears to be Larkin playing Russian roulette with Burke. For what reason?"

Michaels got up from his chair and began to pace. "Rick, that really bothers me. Here you have two very influential people being visited by a former spook now in a prominent, albeit a bullshit position, with top secret access. And he presents them with a crazy video. The thing that keeps me going on this is Burke's background and his history of contacts with violent radicals. You don't change overnight."

"You know," Rick interjected, "You've dug a

little hole for yourself by having Gerosa go into his act, and put a recorder in the cabin. Our footprints better not be on any of this because we are dealing with two high-level people who, if they knew we were behind this, would cut both our nuts off as well as tarnishing the Bureau. God knows the last thing the Bureau needs now is to get slapped around in Congress, particularly since we have a new director."

Their conversation was interrupted as Susan tapped on the door to the office. Before waiting for a response, she walked in as to show Michaels that she had preference over him. A little mind game on her part.

"The Assistant Director wanted this out to the SACs."

She handed him a sealed interoffice envelope and returned to her desk. Dean removed a memo with a Top-Secret stamp on the top and bottom. There was the caution that it should not be disseminated, and used only to be alert if the contents should arise in any ongoing investigation. He glanced at the one paragraph and looked back up at Michaels who was still pacing the room looking at the various awards that Dean had on the wall and on the coffee table.

"What is this Rick, the Dean memorial museum? Without me, half this shit wouldn't be here. I do all the work, and you get the glory."

Dean placed the memo on his desk and looked up. "Eddie, if you had behaved yourself, you could have ended up in this chair, and had all those props around to impress visitors who don't really know it is all bullshit."

Michaels returned to his chair. "No thank you, you keep all the crap. They can be all loaded into a truck that follows your hearse when you check out of here. And then dumped in before the dirt covers you up. For me, I'm happy to retire anonymously, and live where no one will bother me."

Michaels noticed that Dean had read the memo, but did not feel that he should take advantage of their friendship and ask what was so important that it came in a sealed interoffice envelope. Memos usually came unsealed, and the contents rarely had the top secret stamp, which Michaels noticed as Dean extracted the memo.

Dean broke the silence and slid the memo across the coffee table.

"Take a look at this. Little details, something you should put in the back of your head. Who knows what you and Gerosa are dealing with? You never know. Just adhere to the caution."

Michaels read it quickly, filed it mentally, and passed it back. "A little bizarre. Who the hell would have access to sarin around here? Anyway, do I have a green light to continue this case?"

Dean leaned back in his chair. "Not sure what case you are talking about. This meeting never happened."

He got up and extended his hand to Michaels. "Tell Dick that one of these nights I want to come over for Italian. I hear he is a pretty good cook, and with the undercover budget you got for him, he has enough for a good bottle of wine."

As Michaels walked out, he grinned at Susan. They had known each other for many years, and each knew where the other's skeletons were hidden when it came to socializing with office personnel.

"Why the shit eating grin, you smug bastard," Susan smiled. "Haven't seen you in a while now that you became a blue-collar laborer and are spoken for with Nancy."

"One never knows how these things work out." He grinned as he walked away remembering the few trysts they had when they were both younger.

CHAPTER 16

Gerosa's apartment, Pelham Bay, Bronx

"It's your loss. Maybe over the weekend I can try again," Gerosa said sarcastically into his personal cell phone.

"Keep trying, and maybe you will get lucky." It was a Thursday, and Susan Wollman just got home to her apartment from work. Gerosa offered to pick her up and go for dinner somewhere in Manhattan, where he wouldn't run into anyone connected with his undercover role. She knew Gerosa for many years, and dated him for a while before he retired to Florida, and she became Dean's secretary.

"Absence does not make the heart grow fonder, Dickie – more like out of sight, out of mind."

"Ouch, that hurts." Gerosa said. She knew he was kidding, and she would probably see him over the weekend. "Seriously, Dick. I'm beat. Give me a call tomorrow."

"Love ya," was Gerosa's parting comment while hers was "Bullshit."

Gerosa had finished showering, and was deciding what to have for dinner. While eying the contents of his refrigerator, his undercover cell phone rang.

"Hi Dick, it's Annie."

Surprised at the call, he was curious as to why.

"What's up Annie? Why the call?"

"Kieran is at the union hall, and I'm alone staring at the walls. Mind if I come over."

Strange, but what the hell, thought Gerosa, I'll go along with her.

"Well, I'm not doing anything also. Could pick you up in about half an hour." He wanted a reaction.

"No, I'm sick of restaurants. You brag about your cooking. I'll bring some wine. Don't worry, I won't pick anything, and I'll let the liquor store guy pick something that is good. I know the Irish don't really know about red wine."

Gerosa paused. "That's not necessary. Want me to pick you up?"

"No, there is a car service around the corner. I'll be there in about twenty minutes if that is okay with you."

"Sure, see you then" said Gerosa after giving her the address, which he ordinarily would not have done, but the call made him curious. He moved quickly around the small apartment, making sure that anything connected to his case, or any personal items were in the small safe in the bedroom closet. He spread some trade magazines on the coffee table in the living room, and poured himself a double shot of Canadian Club, a drink that Michaels got him into when they worked together. As an afterthought, he put some home repair show on the television. He decided not to call Michaels who would have told him to call it off.

Gerosa thought for a moment before going into the kitchen where there was a partially filled bottle of Chianti and a full one on the counter. He dumped the partially filled one down the drain and grabbed the other unopened one. On his way out the door, he hesitated, and returned to the bedroom where he took his undercover Glock pistol and put it in his car along with his I pad.

A half hour later, Annie Larkin came through the door dressed in a pair of loose herringbone slacks and a light red v-neck sweater that showed the little cleavage that she had. A hint of garlic and simmering filetto di pomodoro sauce greeted her.

"Smells good Dick. So far, you are meeting my expectations."

Somehow, she exuded sex, although Gerosa never considered her a sexy person. *Deliberate or coincidental*, he thought. He was in the middle of preparing a pot of pasta Bolognese and escarole.

"What can I get you to drink?"

"I brought some Guinness and I'll take a large glass, that is if you know how to pour a Guinness correctly. Better more, if you have some beer in the fridge, pour me a black and tan. Any beer will do if you don't have Bass ale."

Gerosa came out of the kitchen and grabbed the keys to his car off the coffee table. "I screwed up Annie. Be back in a few minutes. Going to the liquor store to pick up some Chianti. Pasta is no good without a glass or two of Chianti. Want you to try some. Without giving her a chance to respond, he went out the door, and drove his car around the block. He found a parking space where he fired up his iPad, found the app he wanted, and within seconds, it came up. A split screen appeared showing his bedroom, kitchen, bathroom and living room. Before he moved in, he had four hidden cameras installed in the event that he had any critical meetings in his apartment. Each room also had a hidden microphone. There was a receiver and recorder built into a hidden compartment in his kitchen to memorialize any activity, if Gerosa desired not to delete it daily. *Tech guys did a good job.*

Gerosa hoped his absence from the apartment would generate some activity on Larkin's part that would give him a better understanding of who she was. Up to this point, she was an enigma.

Larkin first appeared perusing some of the magazines on the coffee table. Nothing unusual. Gerosa zoomed in. Her eyes were scanning the living room looking for cameras or a microphone. She did the same in the other three rooms, pretending to just observe the dwelling. Returning to the living room, she paced about, still looking.

Damn, she's good, thought Gerosa surprised. Hope the tech guys did better. He watched as she passed the pinhole camera behind a seascape on the living room wall, one on the ceiling fan in the bedroom, and one coming through a curtain rod in the kitchen. Gerosa smiled knowing that usually someone looking for hidden cameras checks moveable objects like clocks, teddy bears, radios, or computers. *Tech guys did good.*

When she was comfortable that she wasn't being watched, she glanced at her watch. She began to methodically rummage through the furniture looking for anything that might give her a picture of exactly who Dick Gerosa was. Larkin stopped briefly and dialed her cell phone.

"Dick, are you still at the liquor store? If so, get some Baileys for me for after dinner."

"Just got here," said Gerosa as he sat a block away. "Be back in ten."

Gerosa knew the call was bogus. It was placed only for her to know how much time she had for her search.

Larkin moved about the apartment going through drawers, closets, looking under furniture. Even lifting the top of the toilet tank and looking in for a secret compartment. Something up to this point bothered her. Too much money was being thrown around by him. No girlfriend and no wife did not compute with someone who appeared to be a laid-back ladies' man. He never showed up with a date at any of their dinners, and never talked about women. She knew for sure that he was not a homosexual.

Gerosa watched curiously as she went through his personal effects in the bedroom and kitchen, returning each item to its original position. There was nothing there that could compromise him, and he relaxed as he watched ever more curious as to her motives. He suddenly froze as he saw her run her hand through the area between his mattress and bed spring. He was relieved that he had taken his pistol from where he stored it.

It was loaded with an eight-round magazine, but he failed to take a second magazine in the same place. He routinely never took it with him, although the Bureau insisted that he have it.

"If I can't hit anything with the first eight rounds, I'll be in no condition to fire the other eight," he recalled telling Michaels and his firearm instructors, who didn't see the levity.

The unexpected happened as he watched Larkin pull the magazine from under the mattress, examine it, and return it to its position. She rapidly continued her search, found nothing of interest, returned to the sofa, again perusing the trade magazines.

Gerosa gave it another five minutes before entering the condo, bottle of Chianti in hand. Realizing that he didn't have the Bailey's, he apologized.

"They were out of Bailey's but don't worry, I have some black sambuca in the kitchen cabinet. Not as sweet, and you'll like it."

"You're not trying to get me drunk, now are you?" She smiled as she patted the couch cushion next to her on the couch. "Come sit down, that is if you can break away from your cooking."

She and Gerosa made small talk. He sipping his pre-dinner Canadian Club, her drinking her second black and tan as he made trips to the kitchen to check on his Bolognese. The first time she went to the bathroom, he rummaged through her small pocketbook looking for a recorder. *Getting paranoid,* he thought. *Wonder about those loose fitting pants. Maybe I can check them later.* No - Get any thought of that out of your mind.

They ate at a small kitchen table, where he had poured two glasses of Chianti. She had one glass and went back to her Guinness.

"You goin' to join me with another glass?" She smiled. He decided to match her with a glass of wine, although he knew that it was not a good idea. Italians were never as good as the Irish at holding their liquor. He had already put down two CC's.

He turned down her offer to do the dishes, and they returned to the living room where he put on Fox News, hoping to generate conversation regarding her political thoughts. He surmised that from her background, and conversations up to this point, she was a socialist, but gave no indication of a violent nature. The first segment showed inmates at Guantanamo. She came up with the question first.

"What do you think about them? Prosecution, persecution, or let them get the hell out. Is the US making a mistake?"

"Hey, it doesn't affect me. I don't give a shit what they do as long as I have an income."

He felt her eyes on him. Did she expect a different response? That was as generic as could be.

"Tell me more about you, Dick."

Ahh, so now it starts, thought Gerosa. He tried to remain calm despite her find in the bedroom.

"What's there to tell?" Gerosa gave her his scripted background information taken from the person whose identification he had. He figured that it was chancy, but if she told Zorn, and he really wanted to know who he was, he could find out, and his cover would be blown. In which case the bosses of their respective agencies would get together and iron out who was doing what, and for what purpose?

He finished his monologue about himself with "And what about you?"

She gave her scripted story, mostly true except her connection with Zorn and the CIA, and her travel outside of Ireland.

Stalemate thought Gerosa. *Bullshit versus bullshit.*

During a lull in the conversation, Gerosa asked, "When will Kieran be home? Do you have to be there?"

"I told him I was going to the movies in Manhattan and might meet some girlfriends from Ireland, so I would be late. He'll come home bollixed and crash. Won't even miss me." She leaned closer and placed her hand on his knee. Although there was a little stirring in his body, reason preempted passion, unusual for Gerosa. He slowly removed her hand, leaned over and kissed her on the cheek.

"Let's not do something we might regret."

After some more small talk, Gerosa ushered her out the door to an awaiting car service that he had called. Words were exchanged about seeing each other again for a dinner without Kieran. Gerosa knew that would not happen. Time was running out.

Back in her apartment she dialed Zorn's cell phone. "Something's not right with Gerardo. I went there tonight for dinner without Kieran. Very closed mouth about his background, other than some generalities and not that I was going to do anything with him, but I came on a little, and he backed off. The interesting part is that I took a look around when he went out for wine and found an eight-round magazine under his mattress. No gun though."

Zorn paused, trying to make sense of what she said.

"So, what about the come on? Maybe you're not his type. The magazine means that he owns a gun. Maybe legal, but probably illegal. I told you I checked him out. Everything he says pans out. If it makes you feel better, I'll have someone physically go to his address in Florida and make some inquiries."

CHAPTER 17

Pompano Beach, Florida

This was an easy gig for PI Don Jones. Unlike other assignments given to him by Mike Zorn that involved sophisticated surveillance, this was simply a verification of residence. At least that's what the email that he received earlier in the day said. Jones never asked why or any explanation of the cases he investigated for Zorn. He knew Zorn's past, and considered it patriotic to just do as he was directed.

The house was nothing fancy; a small two-bedroom inland from the water in a quiet, well-kept neighborhood.

"What can I do for you?" the middle-aged woman dressed in shorts and a tank top, typical for a full-time Florida resident, asked. Reluctant to open up fully, she talked through the outer screen door. Jones looked formal in a sport coat, tie, and slacks, not his normal working attire.

"Ma'am, I represent Publisher's Clearing

House, and am here to verify the address of Richard Gerardo. I'm not saying that he won anything, but our selection progress has narrowed down one of the many winners to this area of Pompano. So, I just have to verify that he is here."

"I throw all those announcements in the garbage, so I don't know how he can be a winner if he never entered." came the reply through the screen.

"Ma'am, that's only part of it. There are other random selections that we do. Now, it is important that I see Mr. Gerardo to make sure that he has not passed away or that you and he are not divorced because that would eliminate you from any portion of the monetary award, should he be a lucky winner."

"Well mister, my husband Richard and I are very well married, and he would gladly meet with you, but he is out of town and up in New York doing some construction work. Work down here is very slow. Most of the builders and contractors have gone under, as evidenced by the partly built office buildings you can see on route A1A. He hasn't retired yet, and we want to build up our nest egg a little more. I can give you his cell phone. If you want to call him, I'm sure he would be happy to meet with you if you want to go to New York."

Jones took down the number on a small pad. "Just to be sure, and I don't mean to be pushy, but do you have a picture of him around? Just to make sure. It's my job, ma'am. Just have to verify because we are talking about a million bucks here." Jones decided this plain-looking woman would go for it, and Zorn would admire his thoroughness.

"Well, I don't know. I don't know you, but I guess he wouldn't mind. You stay here." She locked the screen door and disappeared, coming back a few seconds later with a framed five by seven photo.

"Took this before he left for New York. Wanted me to look at it every night, so I would miss him." She smiled as Jones quickly made a copy with his cell phone camera.

"Thank you ma'am, and I certainly hope I come by again to present you with a check." A brief smile and he departed. A mile away, he pulled to the curb, went to the end of the contacts on his cell phone, and dialed Zorn.

"Mike – it's your friendly PI from Florida. Checked the residence, spoke to the wife. He is in New York for some construction company in Long Island. She did not recall the name, but gave me his cell phone number. I even got a copy of a picture of him. I'll be texting it to you as soon as I hang up. Here is the cell phone number she gave me."

Zorn saw that they matched the numbers that Larkin had given him earlier.

"Good Don. Send me an invoice."

Zorn sat back in his chair at Goldstone content that Gerardo was in New York, and that all the database checks he had previously done were valid.

"Your hunch worked, Eddie." The middle-aged woman on the phone was the one who answered the door. She was Special Agent Caroline Jensen from the Miami Office of the FBI.

"A PI giving a bullshit story just left after I told him Gerardo was in New York, and gave him his cell number. Also, let him have a copy of the photo you emailed. Mr. and Mrs. Gerardo were great letting us do this, so I gave them $500 of Bu money for their troubles of the past two days. Told them it was a terrorist investigation. What citizen could resist cooperating with the FBI against terrorists?"

Two days earlier, as a result of Larkin's overly questioning of Gerosa, Michaels decided to further backstop Gerosa's undercover role in the event Zorn had someone do a personal visit to the other Gerardo. He put in a call to the Miami office of the FBI.

"Gerry, you got to do this for me," he pleaded with a friend who was now a supervisor. Reluctant at first, the supervisor agreed to send an agent to the Gerardo residence absent any paperwork.

After ending the call with his PI, Zorn waited for the text and seeing the picture, he called Larkin.

"You are getting paranoid Annie. Everything checks out, and Gerardo is in New York according to the wife in Florida. I am looking at a picture of him that came from her. Same person in the one you sent me from your cell. So, he has a personal gun. So what? Most New Yorkers do. Don't get paranoid. Just concentrate on Burke and what has to be done."

"That's still unclear. All I know now is something regarding the Freedom Tower. When will I get more info?"

"You will know when I tell you. Right now, you are getting paid to do what I tell you, and paid very well," was the reply as Zorn hung up the phone.

CHAPTER 18

Industrial area, Yonkers, NY

The rental truck blended in with the commercial vehicles in the large lot behind the strip mall. They were all there to unload goods for the merchants. Oblivious to anything going on around them. The driver glanced at his watch for the fifth time. He again looked at his rearview mirror. The trail car behind him that would take him away after the transfer hadn't moved. He was becoming impatient as he tapped his fingers on the dashboard, and considered making a telephone call to make sure his delivery wasn't cancelled.

It was 4:00 pm, and Kieran Burke had already arrived at Katonah Ave. About to stop at the Piper's, Larkin appeared. She directed him to get into a car service run by one of the locals.

"Where are we going," Burke asked as he watched the stores pass by.

"I hope you have a CDL and can drive a box truck," came the reply from Larkin.

He nodded and remained silent for the remainder of the ride.

"Stop here," Larkin directed the driver to the front of one of the stores in the strip mall. She and Burke got out, and made their way through a local Baskin-Robbins to the rear door, which opened to the back lot. Larkin spotted the truck a short distance away parked near some dumpsters.

She startled the truck driver as she approached the driver's side from the rear. He was looking for a car with two occupants.

"Get out and be on your way. Mike will pay you once we find that everything is in order."

Nothing more was said as Burke got behind the wheel and she into the passenger seat. A Yonkers police car drove slowly through the lot, but paid no attention to the rental truck as it pulled out on to the main road.

Larkin gave the directions as Burke proceeded to the eastern part of Yonkers to a self-storage facility. It was a quiet area off the Deegan Expressway. The rented space had a loading dock and a roll-up door, which would facilitate the unloading of the two crates, each containing two 50-gallon drums each containing two small tanks. As far as Larkin and Burke knew, the drums contained a large quantity of C-4 explosives to be loaded into empty acetylene tanks.

Neither Burke nor Larkin knew the middle-aged man dressed in coveralls who was sitting on a five gallon paint can in front of the roll-up door. His closely cropped crew cut gave him a military appearance, but nothing more to disclose that he was a former Navy diver and demolitions expert with a specialty in welding. He said little as he directed Burke to back the rear of the truck up to the loading platform.

The truck in position, crewcut rolled up the door, and flipped on a light switch illuminating a battery-powered forklift, an acetylene torch, a small toolbox, a water pump and a 25-foot hose. In the rear, lined up against the wall, were eight empty acetylene tanks that he had picked up at a Bronx scrapyard. He had cut the bottoms off preparing for the next step. Crewcut methodically removed each of the four pallets with the forklift, and placed them in the storage space.

"Wait in the truck," he directed Larkin and Burke.

Several minutes passed as crewcut took the crates apart with a crowbar, and seeing the four drums, he piled the wooden remnants into the rental truck, and dismissed Burke and Larkin. The storage space was picked because of its proximity to a storm drain where the water in the drums would go as he pumped it out.

"What was that all about?" Burke asked as the truck headed towards Katonah Avenue. Larkin was silent.

"Park anywhere on the avenue or a side street. Arrangements have been made to have it picked up and returned. Our plan is starting to move. Once they are ready to go, those acetylene tanks that you might have noticed against the wall of the storage space will go to the Freedom Tower. You will take them there and find a storage space until you receive further orders. Steal a large gang box, paint it over and put it up high near the laborers' shanty. Can you do that?"

"Of course. There are gang boxes all over the place down there, and unless they have a lock on them, no one cares. Some of the contractors leave the empty ones when they leave because they are old, or it is too much of a pain in the ass to take it with them."

"Good. You bring in the tanks on a handcart on the weekend, so no one will notice. I'll let you know when. Get started tomorrow working on the gang box."

Burke was surprised at her tone. Different from when they were having a beer, and certainly different from when they were making love. He remained silent until they parked the truck a few blocks away. After texting a location on her cell, she smiled.

"How about a beer at the Piper's?" Content with the day's activity, her mood changed from strictly business to her normal tone, and Burke readily agreed to the beer. This time they sat at a booth instead of on bar stools. Larkin smiled, but was serious.

"Kieran, I know this is starting to go pretty fast for you." She gave a weak smile. "As I said, you will be famous, go down in history, and be responsible for putting a major dent in capitalism by taking apart the ultimate symbol, the Freedom Tower. This is what all our conversations have been leading up to."

Burke thought for a moment.

"Very simple," Larkin said, "The tower will come down. You will be pulled off the roof by a helicopter as the building goes down, and you are whisked away to a waiting aircraft that will take you back to Ireland with a new identity and a briefcase full of cash."

Burke sat silent for a moment. He broke out in a smile. "You forgot the part where you will be meeting up with me in Ireland."

"That's a definite, Kieran. I will know your new name, and will be able to catch up with you after a couple of weeks. You will be staying initially in a bed and breakfast in Ennis, near Shannon airport, and I will meet you there." Larkin smiled through her lie.

"Goddamn, you're good," said Burke as he raised his glass of Guinness in a toast. They were not aware of the change from dynamite to sarin.

It took an hour for crewcut to drain the four drums, and as told to him, each contained two small cylinder tanks, the dimensions of which would let one fit into one of the large acetylene tanks in the rear of the room. He didn't know what was in the cylinders, nor did he care. He was being paid well, and whatever happened after he finished his job was not his concern. He checked to see if the small tank slid into the larger ones. Perfect, with a little room on the sides for what he packed in the large suitcases in the corner of the room. He was now ready to take care of business.

For the following four hours, crewcut packed the eight acetylene eight tanks with the C4 from his suitcase along with the smaller cylinders containing sarin, and welded the bottoms back into place. He stood back and admired his work. The delicate part, which he was skilled at, came next.

He unscrewed the tops of the tanks, exposing a small hole behind which was the packed C4, and inserted a blasting cap. He had eight small altimeters, each powered by a miniature, powerful battery, and set them at sea level, dialed a number from an outdated flip-top phone, after which he punched in five digits. Immediately, each altimeter clicked, and he followed this by testing each one with a voltmeter to ensure that the current coming out would activate the blasting caps.

Crewcut smiled as each one performed as expected. *Damn, he was good.* He punched in another five digits and the current ceased. The altimeters were set to the specific heights that he was given. Their wires were connected to the blasting caps and placed inside the eight tanks. The tops were welded back on. His job was almost done. What they were being used for and by whom was not crewcut's concern.

He pulled his pickup truck to the entrance and removed his equipment, making sure that no debris or fingerprints were left behind. The number he dialed and the five-digit code would later be emailed to an untraceable email address that would be accessed by Zorn's cell phone. A large amount of money would then be wired into crewcut's girlfriend's bank account. He would disappear until his next assignment.

CHAPTER 19

Lodge at Wyndham

"I thought we should get together now rather than wait for next week. Things are coming together, and we have to have an after action plan." Whitaker was nervous as he sat in his usual place in the living room. "I see some potential problems, and want to make sure that when the shit hits the fan, no footprints lead to us."

"What are your concerns?" Kirkland didn't like any glitches. During his career, his decisions were never overturned. He received nothing but praise from the various bar associations, and expected this latest venture to be the same, since it was the most important.

"Mike has been keeping me apprised of what's going on with Larkin and our Irishman, and she has him under control, ready to do her bidding. Our package is in place, although no one knows that we made a switch in the contents midstream. That is good because we don't want anyone getting second thoughts. We just need the packages put at the target, and once that is done, we can pick and choose when it all goes down. Right now, we are sticking with September 12. Everyone expects something to happen on 9/11, but the 12th is better."

"I agree," said Kirkland. "Where are our weak areas? I need to know anything that could go wrong at the last minute." He knew something was on Whitaker's mind, and he wanted it resolved.

Whitaker continued, "Burke is no problem. He will be gone. I'm concerned about the girl. She's done a great job so far, appears to have no allegiance to anyone, just the almighty dollar. But I believe it's dangerous to have her around knowing what she does, what she sees, and what actually happens. It can't directly come back to us. It can through Mike. He's your guy. What do you think?"

"I brought Mike along to where he is. I trust him completely. I might have some questions about his judgment at times, but we can control that. He has done a good job up to this point. I believe that he has cleaned himself pretty well, and no one knows about his connection to the girl. Remember, he is not with the Agency anymore. There is no paper trail regarding his activities. The money he is taking out comes from an unlimited and unaudited fund. It is merely a pittance to what the Agency spends on useless operations."

"One more item," said Whitaker. "Mike has briefed me regarding this guy Gerardo who has been hanging around with the girl and Burke. Came up from Florida to be a super for a contractor on Long Island, and has hired Burke to do some off the books weekend work. Everything seems legitimate. Mike had him checked out by a PI in Florida. Everything fits in with all the database checks. The only thing that bothers me is that he has a wife in Florida, and purports to be single up here."

Kirkland grinned. "Aren't you a little naïve? Guy away from home living in a bachelor pad. So, he puts it out that he is single. Not surprising to me. Is that the only concern that you have?"

"No, Larkin went through his apartment while he was out getting wine, and found a fully loaded magazine under his mattress. That means he has a gun. Something's not right."

Whitaker looked at his watch. "Mike should be here any minute. We can get his thoughts and finalize this whole thing. I just want to get it over with, so things can get moving with my company. I could use a drink." He walked to the bar and poured a straight scotch.

After twenty minutes of watching Fox News on the small flat screen, the door opened and Zorn entered. Before he sat down, he gestured that they move outside.

"Michael, in case you haven't noticed, it is raining out," said Kirkland, "and I do not have an umbrella. Stop with the paranoia and let's get down to business." Zorn reluctantly agreed.

Whitaker put his drink down, sat forward in his chair and began, but was cut off sharply by Zorn.

"Excuse me if I am paranoid. Let's not be too specific in case what we read about the NSA is true. Their computers pick out key words in conversations, and then they go for the whole thing." Kirkland rolled his eyes.

"Let's get started. Ed, tell him what we were discussing."

Whitaker finished his glass of scotch, walked to the bar, and set it down. He turned and directed his attention to Zorn, who had taken a seat on the couch.

"Mike, we have some concerns. The first is A L. She knows too much at this point. Everything except our switch. She's a mercenary, and who's to say she won't sell this information after everything goes down to save her skin if the authorities somehow get to her."

Zorn thought for a moment as to what the judge and businessman wanted to hear. "I don't see her as a liability. If you think she might be, I can take care of that. I have always had contingency plans. There is a way that she can disappear, and I can have someone with her identity fly back to Ireland to make it look like she went home. This has been done in the past."

"I get the point," said Kirkland. "No need to go further." The judge always wanted to distance himself from details.

Zorn grinned. "What else, or can we proceed with the date I gave you?"

"I have concerns about Gerardo," said Whitaker. "Something doesn't add up."

Zorn cut him off. "Ed, I checked him out every which way. The only problem is that he is always around. More so than a normal situation. I attribute that to him wanting to hit on Larkin. The gun is no big deal in the Bronx, but he does throw a lot of money around for a worker."

"Suppose he stumbles onto something as our plan is about to go down?" interjected Kirkland.

Zorn thought for a moment. "I can make something happen that will take him out of the picture for a couple of days, and when he reappears, our plan is over, and K B and A L are gone. Who is he going to talk to and why? He will probably go back to Florida and his wife. What dots could he connect? Let me handle it."

For the next hour, mundane conversation went on, mostly about the world situation and the economy.

"I have to get going so as not to run into too much traffic on the way back. I don't have the luxury of an on-call whirlybird. Don't worry, everything is a go, and I am going to make sure that it works." Zorn grinned as he excused himself and exited.

And if it doesn't work, no one will ever hear from me again, and I will be a new man in Europe with a ton of money that I siphoned out of the Agency, Zorn thought as he got into his SUV.

CHAPTER 20

New York FBI Office

"I don't want to put you in the middle of this, and I will deny everything if this ever gets out. Something big is going on here, and I need your advice."

Michaels placed the miniature recorder on the small coffee table. Before he could push the play button, Dean interjected in a tone that Michaels was unaccustomed to.

"Eddie, I suggest that you stop all of this James Bond bullshit that can get your ass fired in the twilight of your retirement, and can get you and your running mate Gerosa indicted. You capisce?

"Rick, just listen, and then tell me what you think. As far as I am concerned, this recording doesn't exist."

Dean leaned back on the sofa and nodded.

Michaels played the recording that Gerosa the night before retrieved from the cabin.

"Putting the pieces together so far, it appears

they are all in some kind of conspiracy that will come to pass on September 12, day after the anniversary of the Twin Towers coming down. It just doesn't add up. The way the Freedom Tower or Tower 1 as it is known is being built, no amount of dynamite would take it down, and no airplane, even a 747 could replicate what happened on 9/11."

"Eddie, right now you have a respected federal judge on an illegal wire. Also, there is a respected businessman and the New York Homeland Security representative. And this all started because some Irish laborer thought something funny was going on with one of his men. This guy Burke, we know has had a past sympathy to the radical Muslim movement, and hooks up with an Irish gal who also happens to be an Agency asset or at least a former asset. I'd say it is time to bring in the Joint Terrorism Task Force. This info would surely whet their appetite." Dean waited for a reaction.

Michaels stood. "Are you fuckin' crazy? What you said before about indictment definitely would happen. With that asshole left wing attorney general that we have, we would all end up in jail even if we saved the world from destruction. No way is that going to happen. Give me some more time to sort all of this out. How about putting a surveillance team on Burke?"

"Won't happen unless we lay out all the info, and we can't do that. You can try it on your own. Burke has never seen you, but one-man surveillance is close to impossible. What I am very concerned about is that I gather from the conversation we just listened to, Larkin's life could be in danger, and more importantly, Gerosa's. I gather that they just want to remove Gerosa from the picture, make him privy to nothing. Then send him packing back to Florida. It appears that at this point they do not believe that he knows anything to hurt them, and to kill him would create too many problems. If Larkin is killed like it appears that they are planning, no one would really care, and sending someone with her identity back to Ireland would put everything to rest. Tell me, what does Kirkland and Whitaker have to gain by all of whatever they have planned at the Freedom Tower?"

Michaels thought for a moment. "It's more than a couple of right-wing nuts. From the sound of Whitaker's business, although we haven't really fleshed out what it actually does, I would guess there could be some lucrative government contracts if whatever they are doing under the guise of a terrorism act provokes a knee-jerk reaction that puts us into another war. Right now, with all the shit going on in the Mideast, and the conservatives begging for action, whatever is being planned could put public opinion against the current administration, and force it to do something positive."

"That's a possibility. What about Kirkland?"

"That I don't know. Maybe some kind of patriotic ideology."

Michaels got up. "Regarding Larkin, I have an idea how we keep her safe, and as far as Dick goes, he knows what is on the recording and will be cautious in the future." He paused as he reached the door. "I'll keep you advised."

Dean moved to his desk. "In the old days, I would join you on surveillance, but in my present position, that is out of the question. Then again, let me know your plans, maybe I could join you." Michaels nodded and grinned as he left.

Gerosa was putting together a couple of salami and provolone sandwiches and finishing off the couple of shots of espresso that he had for breakfast when Michaels came through the door of the apartment.

Gerosa took the ever present towel that he used when preparing food from off his shoulder.

"It was a bad idea for you to have a key to this place. No telling who might be here this hour of the day dressing to go home."

"You should be so lucky." Michaels went to the refrigerator and popped open a beer. "Just spoke with Dean, and he wanted to turn this all over to the Task Force."

Gerosa stopped polishing a wine glass and looked at him. "Is he nuts?"

"I told him our thoughts, and he reluctantly agreed. Wouldn't give us a surveillance team. Said

I could surveil Zorn. Big deal."

Gerosa smiled. "Okay, why the shit eating grin," asked Michaels.

"I'm one step ahead of you. Last night, I went through all the info you gave me on the flash drive. I got Zorn's address on Bell Road in Scarsdale and took a ride and put one of the new tracking devices on his SUV. In addition to the battery, I was able to run a direct power supply from the lights. Couldn't get under the hood in the driveway, so the battery would get a boost whenever he turns on his lights. Best I could do. Can bring him up on the computer or my cell phone, usually within 30 yards of where he is. What's an illegal tracking device mean on top of an illegal wire?"Gerosa grinned, cut the salami hero in half and passed it to Michaels as they listened to the conversation again.

"What's your take?" Michaels asked Gerosa.

"We've got a little over a week. We can track Zorn and hope for the best. I think it is now time to do something proactive, I can take care of myself as far as that veiled threat on the tape. I'm concerned that we don't have the whole picture at this time. What do you think about approaching Larkin?"

"We don't have enough money to buy her loyalty," answered Michaels. "What about the threat of her disappearing? What would be Larkin's reaction to that?"

"I don't know," said Gerosa as he grabbed a

beer. "Let's give it a day."

CHAPTER 21

Goldstone Office, NYC

Zorn arrived early for his afternoon meeting with Annie Larkin and had rehearsed the script he would use to finalize the plans for September 12. It was getting close, and he did not want to disappoint Kirkland and Whitaker. More important, he saw a bright future for him in government if all went well. Right now, the key was Larkin. This was the biggest caper of her life. It had to go smoothly.

Larkin was punctual. Zorn buzzed her through the secure door of the small office. There were no perfunctory greetings, as she assumed her seat in front of the desk. She was all business.

"Is everything in place for next week on your end?" Zorn asked.

"From my end, yes. Burke will do anything I want. All he knows now is that he will be working with dynamite to do something at the Freedom Tower. He has worked with it before and seems very comfortable. I told him his escape plan and he had no questions. All I need to know is when you want the tanks removed from the storage space. We only have one weekend until the target date, so he will have to move on this Saturday and Sunday. He should have no problem."

"What about getting through the gate?" came the response. "Do they check everything going in?"

"Yes, but only during the week. They usually have someone checking the delivery trucks, checking bills of lading, physically going through the trucks, viewing the underside with mirrors, etc. to make sure they are legitimate deliveries, and are delivering what they claim on the bill of lading. On the weekend, there are only the twelve dollar an hour security guards who just go through the motions of scanning ID cards and opening the main gate for them. There are no deliveries scheduled for the weekends, and a hand truck going through with a couple of acetylene tanks would cause no concern."

"What about the other laborers who are there who might see him?operation"

"There are only a few working this weekend on an early shift; coming in around 6:30 am and leaving around 1:30. I'll have Kieran try to do it all on Sunday after 2. Should be no problem."

Zorn seemed content so far. "Where does he store them?"

"We are fortunate that the laborers' shanty is close to the top floor. They are at 80 now, which is only a short distance to the elevator shafts. Kieran will not draw any attention by going to and from the shanty. The hoist operators don't care who or what they are carrying up and down to the various floors. All they are concerned about is their time and a half for working the weekend."

"What about the storage up to D-Day?"

"I'm ahead of you Michael," answered Larkin. "Each trade has several gang boxes in which they keep tools, supplies or whatever. If you walked the site, you would see many, some with the name of the company painted on the side and some nothing. Kieran has one in sight that appears to have been abandoned by one of the companies that left the site for whatever reason. He already moved it to a secluded area, and once I direct him to bring the tanks in, he will relocate it to an area near the shanty. The box can hold all of them; the only potential problem would be if one of the safety people saw him. Acetylene is supposed to be stored in locked metal cages with signage on it. He doesn't anticipate that any safety people will be working on Sunday. This has all been planned out. He is ready to go."

Zorn knew from experience that Larkin paid attention to detail. That made her a good operative, which brought the next question.

"How about the escape plan for him. How is a helicopter going to get through after the dynamite goes off?" Larkin wanted this last detail.

"I've taken care of that. Someone, whose

identity you do not need to know has access to Teterboro Airport, only a few miles away. When we are about an hour to go, he will steal a helicopter, and proceed to a secure location where the ID number on the chopper will be changed. Then to the tower. With all the news and police helicopters, he will be able to get Kieran out without causing suspicion. They will think it is a commercial helicopter doing a heroic act by saving someone. He will then be dropped at Westchester County Airport, where he will be given a new identity. A fight to Fort Lauderdale, then on the Shannon. All ready to go."

What a line of BS, thought Zorn, but she went for it, and I'm sure he will. Zorn knew it was a moot point. The rapid spread of the sarin gas would eliminate Burke immediately.

"What about me?" asked Larkin. "Where do I go? What is my plan to get out of here? I know I went over this before, but I want to hear it again?"

Zorn sensed some hesitation. Larkin survived for so long because she was smart, evidenced by the way that she studied and applied suggestive behavior with Burke. She was also cautious in her dealings with Zorn, and kept a low profile ensuring anonymity in the Katonah Avenue community. But he was smarter.

"Annie, a couple of hours before this goes down, someone will call you to arrange a meet with you in a secure location. He will give you a package. In it will be a new identity, airline tickets to Ireland and a substantial sum of money. You will take off from Westchester County, go to Miami, then on to Dublin. After that, you are on your own."

"Michael, let's be specific. How much money?"

"I am working that out now. Probably half a million." He made this figure up because he knew it would never come to pass.

"Bullshit. I could never take that much money aboard an airplane. It would be seized, and I would be locked up for questioning. Let me give you my terms. I want $10,000 in cash that I can hide in different places in my handbag, luggage and wherever else it might go undetected. I also want $500,000 wired to a bank account that I will open in the Central Bank of Ireland in Dublin, and I want it done the day before the target date. I will give you the account number when you are ready to make the transfer." Larkin sat back, and waited for an answer as he studied her movements.

Zorn thought for a moment. *I underestimated her. She thinks this is an Agency operation. Therefore, money is no object. He leaned forward and smiled.*

"Annie, you drive a hard bargain. How can I negotiate at this stage of the game? Let me work things out. Let's consider it done. The only thing is that the Central Bank of Ireland is no good. I will have to do it through the Barclays Bank on Wilson Street in Dublin. The Agency has a central account there under a cover name through which millions have been funneled in the past. Actually, it was set up by the Agency through one of the high-ranking managers who knows whose money it really is. Moving money from that account to an account will be easy if it goes to an account in the same bank. No questions will be asked if the money is moved out quickly to wherever you want it to go. You can't open up an account yet because you do not have your new identity. I will do that for you. You can call the bank to verify when you get the package on the morning of the 12th. Okay?"

Larkin was thinking how this could backfire on her. "If that is an Agency account, couldn't they just as well take the money out after the operation before I get to it?"

Zorn had already planned for this contingency. "No, not at all. It would raise too many eyebrows. Some of the lower-level employees could not remove the money from the account unless it is directed by you. So, the answer is no. Also, you will have a three-hour layover in Miami. During that time you can call to verify that the amount has been transferred. Listen, I've trusted you this far. You should trust me. It is not my money; it is the Agency's, so it means nothing to me. The only consideration is the amount. If you had wanted more, I probably would have had to take a stand, but your figure is within the parameters for which we planned. Are you on board with this?"

Larkin reluctantly nodded, although Zorn could see that she was still mapping it all out.

"So, if there is nothing more, let's get moving. We will not meet before the 12th. Someone that morning will give you your new identity and plane tickets. He will call you early to set a time and place to meet. An account will already be opened in your new name. If anything comes up before then, get me on my cell. From this point on, get a burner phone. I will do the same. That is the way we will communicate.

"Call this number," Zorn passed a folded piece of paper to her, "Leave the number of your burner phone. I will call you with mine."

Larkin nodded. She rose slowly digesting what Zorn had just told her attempting to pick holes in his plan; basically, how she could get screwed out of her money and her exit. Zorn could see her apprehension, smiled slightly, and nodded before she made her way to the door.

She has been a good operative over the years, perhaps the best I ever handled. I'd hate to see her eliminated, but this is the real world. The question is how? He thought as he leaned back in his swivel chair. I can't get her the money I promised, but can set up the charade, which will only be good until she checks her account. Then it is over.

It was late afternoon. Larkin was waiting on a bar stool, avoiding the locals who regularly tried to hit on her. She went to the Piper's to meet Burke after she left Zorn, and as she waited, she mused how Burke accepted orders easily after only a few months of her coaching, and on this Saturday before September 12, he was ready to move the eight acetylene tanks. Just needed the orders.

Burke felt pretty good about himself as he walked briskly down Katonah Avenue. Whatever Annie's plan was, it was coming together, and he was a part of it. From what he knew, cylinders filled with dynamite would be dropped down the elevator shafts, explode, cause confusion, and kill several people. This would send a message to capitalism that their war against Muslims was far from over. Their so-called impenetrable symbol was, in fact, vulnerable. He would be whisked away by helicopter, and within twenty-four hours be back in Ireland with a lot of money. *Damn good operation. The boys over there will be proud of me when it comes out.*

As he entered, Larkin could tell that Burke was in good spirits, waiting for his next order. He pulled up a stool next to hers, kissed her on the cheek, and ordered a Guinness.

"When do you want me to deliver the cylinders, and what time do they go down the shaft on the twelfth?" he asked as he looked at one of the televisions showing an Irish football game.

"This Sunday, you move the cylinders at whatever time you think is best. Currently, the time for the 12th will be at 9:00 am. This is subject to confirmation, and possible change as it has to be coordinated with the helicopter. Nine was selected because that is when the number of people coming and going from the entrance to the

PATH trains is at their maximum. I'll confirm that."

Larkin reached into her pocketbook and pulled out a small, outdated flip-top phone. "Use this from now on. The number is scribbled on the inside along with my new number."

CHAPTER 22

Gerosa's apartment

Gerosa knew that he had to move quickly. He listened to the tape several times, but came to the same conclusion. He had nothing definitive, and he could speculate as much as he wanted. Something big was going to happen. If it did, not only would there be a catastrophe, but when all the dust settled, he could go to jail for several reasons, all relating to his freelancing. He now even regretted getting involved with Michaels, although he had to admit that he loved the thrill of the chase as long as it all ended in his favor. In addition to the tape, Larkin and Kieran blew off the last two dinners, although he did have a couple of conversations with her suggesting that they get together again without Kieran.

Gerosa was impetuous, sometimes to his own fault. This time was no different. It was early afternoon, and he was supposed to be working. He figured that Larkin may also be working or whatever she did during the day. He dialed her number hoping to get her.

Gerosa unblocked his caller ID, so she would know it was him. He was concerned that she might not answer if the call came up private. She answered on the third ring,

"Hi Dick, what's going on? I'm kind of busy, so can you be brief?" She didn't want to create suspicion by not answering the call, so she thought it best to give him some bullshit story.

"Annie, I want to see you as soon as we can get together; that is without Kieran." She thought it unusual and didn't know whether it was his prurient interest or something else, but with all that would be going on, she thought it best to go along with him, find out what was on his mind, and get him out of the way for the next several days. This included keeping him happy sexually if that's what he wanted.

She tried one more time, "Dick, I'm really busy, can we make this a week from now?'

"No, I really want to see you tonight." His voice had a sense of urgency. She hoped that it did not have anything to do with her impending plans. She thought for a moment. "When and where, Dick?"

"Can you take a car service to my apartment, and be here around five, or I can pick you up?"

"I don't know. Kieran will be home by then. He expects us to have dinner at the Piper's. Why don't you join us?" She pressed again to blow him off.

"Tell him you have to meet some friends in Queens to go to a movie or whatever. Meet him early and get a few Guinness in him. He won't care after that."

She thought for a minute, and knew she could easily get rid of Kieran, but what was the urgency.

"How much time?"

"Annie, I went to spend a little time. I'll have food and some wine. Even got some Guinness for you."

She thought for a moment. *The only way to find out if there is a problem is to go.*

"Will do. See you then." She thought for a while about calling Zorn, and let him know about the call, but decided that that would be overreacting. Whatever he wanted, she would accommodate him. She had noticed in the past how he looked at her, and how there was a touchy-feely moment when she had dinner at his apartment. Underneath it all, she liked him and found him attractive.

Eddie Michaels' last words before he hung up the phone with Gerosa were "You are fucking crazy. I am going to retire in a few months, and now I'm in the middle of this crazy caper. I'll be there as I have been in the past, but I may put in my early retirement papers before I leave."

"Remember Eddie, you called me" said Gerosa as he hung up the phone smiling.

When Larkin arrived, Gerosa had already

downed a Canadian Club to relax. A bottle of Chianti was on the table set for two, and a large pot on the stove slowly brewed chicken cacciatore, the aroma of which filled the small apartment. Larkin hadn't planned on dinner. Her first impulse was to get out quickly once she found out the urgency of his call, and to make sure that it had nothing to with her upcoming plans. Now that she was there, her mood changed, and she considered it a time to relax because the next few days would be hectic.

Gerosa greeted her with a kiss on the lips, quite a change from the peck on the cheek she gave him the last time that she was there.

Dinner was uneventful. They finished the bottle of Chianti as they made small talk about Ireland and his landscaping business. Gerosa wanted her lucid for what was to come. He refrained from opening a second bottle, although he believed that some of his best undercover work came after he had a little buzz on. Contrary to medical reports, he believed that alcohol helped him make better decisions.

Michaels had been a block away when the car service pulled up. As soon as Larkin entered, he moved his SUV close to the apartment, and adjusted the volume of the radio frequency receiver on the front seat. Gerosa's conversation with Larkin was coming in clear. The recorder part of the receiver was turned off, as none of what was to transpire would be evidentiary.

After dinner, they went to the living room

couch. Gerosa took out a bottle of black Sambuca from a makeshift liquor cabinet.

"Better than the clear buca, not as much sugar," Gerosa said as he poured two small snifter glasses. He raised his in a mock toast. "Cienz An. That means you should live to be a hundred or should I say Sláinte?"

Something intrigued her about him, but she had to stay focused on the plans for the next few days.

"Okay Dick. What do you have on your mind? I've been around the block a few times. I know this whole setting is something more than a casual dinner, all this not wanting to have Kieran around and a private dinner. What's up? If you are hitting on me, I'm flattered, but not tonight. I've got a lot on my mind." She finished the glass of Sambuca in a couple of gulps, and moved towards Gerosa on the couch. She pulled him close to her and kissed him on the lips for a couple of seconds, and then pushed him away.

"Not tonight Dick, but in the near future. Right now, I have to get out of here."

"Sorry about that," said Gerosa.

That was what Michaels was waiting to hear. He was wondering why all the bullshit from Gerosa leading up to this, but that was the way he always worked. When Gerosa was with Michaels on the Drug Enforcement Task Force, and he was buying a kilo of heroin as an undercover, it always had to involve an expensive dinner, a lot of wine, and bullshit not connected to the matter at hand. Some things don't change.

Larkin started to dial a car service with her cell phone. "Dick, I'll wait outside. Need some air to clear my head." Gerosa rose with her. He stopped her dialing before she could finish when the door opened.

"Who the fuck are you?" asked Larkin as Michaels entered.

"Dick, who is this creep? A friend of yours?" She was surprised when he did not immediately answer. He just grinned as she glanced back and forth at Gerosa and Michaels, and suddenly felt alone.

"Come on Annie, sit back down. You don't have a choice." Gerosa motioned her towards the couch, and moved to the side to accommodate Michaels who had yet to say a word.

Several thoughts went through Larkin's mind as to what this was all about. She wanted to make sure she had an answer for anything that got thrown at her. She was confident that even if this had something to do with what was going to happen, she had all the answers or at least Zorn would, and she had no compunction about throwing out his name if necessary. After all, he was with Homeland Security, previously with the CIA, and she believed that she had immunity.

Michaels reached into his windbreaker and pulled out his FBI credentials. Without saying a word, he presented them to her. She studied them, and turned to Gerosa.

"So, what is this all about? If you don't mind, I'm getting out of here. There is someone you can speak with that can answer any questions that you might have regarding me. She pulled out her cell phone and began dialing Zorn's number.

"Not yet." Gerosa grabbed the phone from her hand. "I belong to the same club he does." He looked at Michaels, "And we've worked together for years. We're here to save your ass. In turn we want you to work for us."

Larkin heard that pitch before. That is how the CIA recruited her. She knew the drill. But she wasn't about to fold her hand until she knew that they had all the winning cards. She decided to be aggressive.

"Fuck off. Give me my goddamn phone. Unless you have some kind of warrant, I'm outta here."

As she started to rise off the couch, Gerosa grabbed her by the arm and pulled her down. "Annie, I always liked you. Right now we have something better than a warrant. We have a get out of jail free card and a save your ass card. Now just sit back and shut up. We can talk after you hear what we have."

Michaels pulled a miniature recorder from his jacket, placed it on the table in front of them, and hit the play button. The tape was edited to only include the important three minutes where Zorn talked about eliminating her. They would play the rest for her later when this part sunk in, and he felt that he could trust her.

Gerosa did the talking. "Annie, we know where this took place. We know the players. We just don't know the screenplay. Now you have a couple of options; you can tell us what is going on, or you can walk out the door, and call Zorn like you were going to. All that would do is expedite the process of having you, as he said – eliminated. And he has the wherewithal for doing that. He was a rogue CIA agent and somehow got himself the Homeland Security job where he has access to everything he wants."

Larkin was quickly computing all of her options and tried one more bluff. "I get it. You guys think you are onto something and think that I can help you. So, you have your lab guys insert some language that didn't exist into a conversation. Why don't you take your little tape recorder and shove it up your ass." She stared at Gerosa as she looked for a reaction.

Gerosa had played this game before with wise guys and drug dealers, and knew he had her. He grinned slightly as he leaned back on the couch.

"You know, Annie, I really do like you. If you think Eddie and I are wasting our time with a bullshit story, you are wrong. If you walk out that door now, there is no way we can protect you. I'll bet that whatever is going on is almost done, you were promised a large sum of money and a new identity – typical Agency stuff. If you believe that, then you also believe in the tooth fairy. Go ahead, there's the door."

Larkin leaned back into the couch. "What's in this for me? What if I give up a secret government operation? You guys all work for the same government."

"Annie, listen to me." Gerosa rose from the couch, and took a few paces before looking at her. "This is some kind of rogue operation in the Agency. Despite what you see in the James Bond movies, this government doesn't go around killing people for any reason. Give us what you have. The best I can do is ensure that you will not be part of any criminal scheme. More important, we'll keep you alive. After that, I can't guarantee anything."

Larkin thought for a moment, and made her decision. "Okay Dick. Play me the full conversation, and I'll fill in the blanks, and tell you what I know." She had no idea who the other two people were, and wanted to know.

"We won't do that now. You are not in the catbird seat, we are. You don't ask the questions or give directions, we do. Just start talking. We will determine if what you are saying is true, and whether you stay or go out the door." Gerosa knew that there was no way she was leaving, even though they had no legal reason to hold her.

For the next two hours, Larkin detailed partially what she was involved in, paying attention to details, and often repeating herself, leaving enough out to keep them guessing, and only as much as she could get away with.

She wanted to convince them that she was sincere, but she wanted to hold back some bargaining chips. No notes were taken. Michaels and Gerosa agreed that they did not want reams of paper generated because from what they believed up to this point, there can't be any judicial proceedings. How, when and where this would all be resolved was yet to be determined.

As Larkin talked, she gave as much as she believed would get her out the door, and held back much of what had occurred, and what she knew. She was a pro at this. She knew that there might come a time when she might have to change allegiance again if she could somehow get around the death threat. She went into her relationship with Zorn, told them about Burke, how he was an instrument in what Zorn was doing, but said that she was not privy to the end game. She omitted the latest developments with the tanks and bringing them on the Freedom Tower site.

Gerosa's mind was in overdrive. He knew she was not going to give up everything, just enough to make new friends, and get her out the door. He decided to bluff.

"Annie, stop the bullshit. Let's hear the rest of the story. I didn't fall off the turnip truck, and have been around more than you. A bullshitter knows when he is getting bullshitted." He played the role well.

She moved her face close to his and went eye to eye. "Why would I lie now? I just want to know

191

what you are going to do to protect me. Do I get protection? Do I get a big sum of cash to get out of town?'

"That's not the way it works," said Gerosa, "We will protect you as best we can, but from now on you work for us. We find out what is going to happen. Then you will be a witness, and we'll put you in the Witness Protection Program. You live happily ever after."

Larkin knew that the only way out was to agree with anything. "Okay, I'll work for you, but no wire. Zorn is always suspicious. When I meet him in his office, I believe he has countermeasures in place to detect any transmitters or recorders. He is very cautious. I will try to get as much info as I can, and will call you every day."

Michaels and Gerosa knew that she wasn't telling everything, but they had pushed her as far as they could at this time. Gerosa reached into his pocket, and pulled out an outdated flip-top burner phone.

"Use this to call every day around four when Kieran is working. We will tell you when and where to meet next. Keep it with you at all times, and we will call you immediately if we believe that you are in any imminent danger. If you find yourself in a dangerous position, hit the star key. It will put a call through to us, and also give us your location in the event we have to bail you out of something." He handed her the phone, and told her Michaels would drop her off a block away from

Katonah Avenue.

"Annie, one more thing. If anything is going to happen, we believe it will be in the next few days as nine eleven is in only four days away. If I were to guess, I would say that is the date. So get to work, and find out what is going to happen."

Larkin knew they didn't believe her, but had no other option, but to let her go. She turned as she went out the door.

"I'd like to say I had a wonderful evening, and end it with a kiss goodnight, but I haven't."

Michaels grinned as he caught Gerosa's eye. He walked her to his car, opened the passenger side door, and let her in.

"Always the fucking gentleman," she said before slamming the door closed.

Gerosa reached under the couch, pulled out a miniature receiver and recorder, flipped a switch and heard the engine start, and Larkin tell Michaels the best place to drop her off.

A friend in the lab said that the transmitter in the phone he gave her was voice activated. The battery would last forty-eight hours, and the max distance was about half a mile.

"Jesus, Dick. Now they can add an illegal wire to the bunch of other charges that we are going to go away for" were Michaels words when Gerosa told him about the phone.

"Not gonna happen," was Gerosa's answer.

Annie Larkin looked out the window of the

car as the homes sped by, but she saw nothing. She was going over the last two hours, and was quite proud of the way she handled what could have been a disaster. She gave them enough to keep them happy, but left out specifics. In a matter of a couple of days, her job will be done, and she will make sure that she doesn't get hurt. They gave her a good heads up, and she had to give up very little. The question she had was who Zorn was talking with when he mentioned that she could be eliminated. Were they the ones behind this? Who would benefit by such a disaster? High-level government? Maybe? But she now knew enough to cover her ass when she was around Zorn, play out whatever was in motion, and make sure she got the money, and a way out of the whole mess. Maybe Zorn was just bullshitting whomever he was talking to. Maybe she could even double-cross Gerosa, and lay out what occurred to Zorn.

Michaels pulled the car to the curb on McLean Avenue just short of Katonah.

"You can walk from here. I don't want to get too close." Michaels looked at her before she got out.

"Think this one out, Annie. Your life is in the balance here. You can jerk us around a little, which I believe you did, and it will not have a happy ending for you. Or you can play on the winning team." He waited for a reaction.

"Hit the door latch," she said as she tried to get the door open. "I'll play your game." The door lock clicked, and she got out and walked to Katonah Avenue, looking at her watch and finalizing a bullshit story as to where she spent the night with her friends in case Burke was still up when she got to the apartment.

CHAPTER 23

FBI Office

"I don't know why I ever listened to you two. Right now, I am knee deep in shit that you got me into. And you tell me Larkin only has a few details of what is going to happen." Dean was peering over his reading glasses as he leaned forward on his desk.

"I know she only gave us half a story, but it was a gamble," said Michaels, "At least I believe she is now on our team."

"Don't count on it." Dean removed his glasses and leaned back as he thought. He looked over at Gerosa.

"Well, you are never at a loss for words. What do you think?"

Gerosa smiled. "I think we are in a good position."

Dean rolled his eyes. "Jesus, the only guy who always has a half a glass full, not a half empty one thinks we are in a good position." He looked at

Michaels. "I'm dying to hear this one. Go ahead," he said as he shifted towards Gerosa.

"So far nothing about all this has been put on paper, but something has to be done quickly. I think we all agree that something big is going to happen on September 11th, the only problem is that we don't know what. We know that there is a federal judge involved with a high-powered businessman, and a former rogue CIA agent. No one would believe what we know up to now, so to turn this over to the Terrorism Task force would only bog things down. September 11 would come, and whatever was going to happen would happen. Then we would all be under the gun for several reasons. My idea is to put a legal mike in the cabin, and see what develops."

"How?" Dean, who is usually mild-mannered started to show signs of irritation. After all, it was his career that was on the line. Michaels could retire, and Gerosa was only a contract employee, one that he had approved on pure bullshit.

Michaels began pacing. "This is what I think we can do, and it will all be legit. First, everyone is on pins and needles now that the anniversary of September 11th is coming up, so I think any legal processes will be expedited if they have anything to do with a possible terrorist act. That being said, I have Judge Roland McHugh in mind. Former FBI agent, very conservative, and has given the Bureau almost everything we wanted regarding search or arrest warrants. Is also very secretive. So, here's my plan. I open up Annie Larkin as an informant. I can use her information as probable cause to put a legal microphone in the lodge. Naturally, everyone will be antsy because there is a judge involved, but they also know if they turn the request down and something happens, the blood is on their hands. I can call Ron Siano, our favorite Assistant United States Attorney, and we can work on the affidavit today. You can alert the tech guys."

Dean thought for a moment. "I don't know why I listen to you, but go for it. We can at least say that we did what we could, should there be a terrorist incident. One question – suppose our guys find the recorder that Dick put in. Then what?"

Gerosa already had the answer. "I'll go with them as part of the entry team and take it out."

Dean stood up. "Are you crazy? It's going to be hard enough to push this through the system. Now you want to be part of an installation. Did it ever occur to you that you are retired? If you weren't, you wouldn't be part of the unit, and you know how they don't want interlopers butting in on any of their operations."

"Rick, you and Jim Nelson go back a long time. I'm sure you can convince him. The alternative is that they go in, and there is a slight chance they will not find the recorder, but then again, they are very thorough and probably will. Then what?"

Dean paced about weighing his options. "Okay, I'll see what I can do. Right now, because of you two, I am in deep, and slowly going under. Go ahead with your harebrained scheme. We can all meet in Florida when we get fired unless the venue happens to be Leavenworth."

Michaels went to the phone on the coffee table. He dialed Siano's number. "Ron, this is Eddie Michaels. Can you come up here this morning? We want to put in an expedite wire. I don't want to go down there as it is very sensitive, and don't want anyone else besides the judge to be privy to the information."

After a pause, "Thanks Ron, see you in an hour."

Michaels hung up the phone. "Let me get going on opening Larkin's informant file. Thanks, Rick."

Dean shook his head as Gerosa and Michaels left the room.

Siano arrived on time, and had some doubts about putting together an affidavit that at best was flimsy.

"Eddie, how long have you been dealing with this so-called informant? Look, I'm not trying to be a pain in the ass, but I have to make sure this not only flies now, but will hold up in court later if there are any arrests. And, as you well know, the law as it is written today directs us to notify any people who were intercepted on a wire ninety days after it is shut down. If nothing comes up to meet our expectations, can you imagine the backlash from a federal judge? You can retire, I can't. I would probably be banished to handling civil matters."

"Ron, you got to trust me on this one. We have been tracking the informant's activities for the last month, including telephone calls, and she has been meeting with this guy, Michael Zorn. We confronted her, and she agreed to cooperate. She specifically said that she has been dealing with Zorn, arranging something under the guise of national security. She lives with a laborer who works at the Freedom Tower construction site. He is a player in whatever is to be done, but she won't know until the last minute."

"It's a bit of a quantum leap to take this to a hunting lodge in Wyndham that is owned by a judge, and I might add, a prominent one."

"We know Zorn has gone there regularly, and met with Judge Kirkland and a high roller in the business of getting government contracts."

Siano stopped writing. "How do we know that they discuss something in the lodge in furtherance of causing a national disaster?"

Michaels knew that this was the one hurdle that they had to overcome, so he stretched some of his so-called informant information.

"Actually, my informant said that Zorn told her that he goes there every so often to discuss what is going to go down on September 11, and that the main player in this is a federal judge. We checked ownership of the lodge. It is owned by Judge Robert Kirkland. We also know that he takes a personal helicopter there every other weekend, and travels with a fellow member of the prestigious Westchester Hall Country Club, Edmund Whitaker. Records of Westchester Trans Copter will confirm this. A source from the County Police gave us this info." He waited for a reaction from Siano.

"You know, Eddie, you put me in a real awkward position. If I don't do this, and shit happens, I'm the scapegoat."

"Sorry Ron, but that is what I wanted to do."

Siano shook his head. "You know I have to run this by my division chief at the office. Not sure whether he will buy it or not."

Michaels grinned. "Now you have him in the same position. He approves, or if he doesn't, it's in his lap if something happens. It takes it off your plate."

Siano nodded. "One more obvious question. Why don't you follow all the players, take it down before it happens or deliberately blow the surveillance to cause them to back off on whatever they are going to do?"

Michaels was prepared for this. "We could do that, but ultimately, we would have one person. There would be nothing to put together a conspiracy, and it would be classified as a lone-wolf action. The judge and Whitaker would be free to plot again."

"What makes you think they will be there on or about September 11 because I have to write in the duration, and if this is only for September 11 or a day or 2 after?"

"Ron, I can't say for sure, but put it this way, if there is some big event being planned, and this year the eleventh falls on a Sunday, they will probably want to see the fruits of their endeavors on the television at the lodge, and celebrate their accomplishments. So run the coverage through Monday or Tuesday. Sunday raises the question as why would they want something to happen on a Sunday when no one is working unless it is just to make a statement, and keep collateral damage being human life to a minimum? I think this is bigger than that. From what I'm getting, the more the damage, human life or otherwise, the more advantageous it is for whatever their cause is. Include the coverage up to Tuesday or Wednesday if you can do it."

"Okay," said Siano. "I'll have this done by the end of the day, and see if I can get in front of our favorite judge by this evening."

The Special Operations Unit, the SOU, never had a contract worker on an installation of a covert microphone, and the head of the unit was always told the background of the case that they were supporting. Following the meeting in Dean's office, Jim Nelson received his call.

After exchanging the usual pleasantries, Nelson knew something out of the ordinary was up. "Okay, Rick, you can now give me the 'by the way', and get straight to the point."

"Jim, I need a special favor, and need I remind you of how you got into your position?" During the past five years, it was Dean who came up with the cases wherein he used Nelson's talents, and later whispered in the Assistant Director's ear that they should consolidate all the special operations such as the technical, surveillance and air units into a separate division, and make Nelson the head. Dean didn't want to play this card, but he didn't want to waste time debating an issue either.

"I need an emergency installation of a mike in an upstate cabin. I want you to take along Dick Gerosa. You remember him from the drug cases."

"No, Rick, that is out of the question. I don't care what you have."

Dean cut him short. "Jim, take my word on this. He is involved in something that borders on terrorism. I brought him in on a case that Eddie Michaels has, and it has developed into something bigger than I thought it would. The microphone is necessary to prevent something that we think will go down on 9-11 or shortly thereafter. Gerosa is an integral part of this, and can facilitate things for you. Should something go wrong without him, it's on your plate. If he goes, it is on mine. Understand?"

Nelson was relatively new at his position but had the nerve, and the ability to circumvent Bureau rules when necessary. He also knew that Gerosa and Michaels were a bit unorthodox, but were solid agents who had good track records.

"Okay, Rick. I will personally handle this with a handpicked team. Tell Gerosa to call me, and get me the court order as soon as possible."

"Can't do," answered Dean. I'll have to hold on to it, and you have to trust me that it is good. It is too sensitive to be floating around the office. If you want, you can come to my office and look at it."

"Okay, I'll have it your way. By the way, who's the target in this, Al-Qaeda, an Arab, Pakistani or an Afghan?"

"Rick smiled on the other end, "None of them – a federal judge and a wealthy businessman," and hung up.

"What the fuck?" Nelson said into a dead line.

CHAPTER 24

Hunting Lodge in Wyndham

Jim Nelson and Dick Gerosa made small talk in the lead vehicle as they made their way up the New York State Thruway towards the turnoff to Wyndham. Behind them was a panel truck with two of Nelson's tech agents. It carried all the equipment necessary to install a microphone in an out of the way cabin, and transmit any conversations back to a special room at an offsite location maintained by Special Operations. A third vehicle followed; an old pickup truck with some landscaper's equipment in the rear. It would be placed blocking the only road into the lodge with engine trouble. For Gerosa and those in the van, they would park in the lot of the Wyndham Country Club. There was still construction going on, so their vehicles would blend in even though it was late evening.

"Did you do your homework?" asked Nelson, presuming that Gerosa did.

"Regarding the targets, one was sitting today, one was midtown according to his GPS, and the third we couldn't get a location on, but be assured that he is probably at his workplace or sitting in his country club bar."

Nelson had scoped the cabin location on a map, and knew the general direction, but let Gerosa take the lead believing that he had most likely been there before, and probably had made a key to the place. He was right.

"Wait for my signal," said Gerosa as they reached the tree line surrounding the cabin. He quietly made his way to the front door, checking the windows along the way to ensure there was no one inside. All seemed set to go until he used his small LED flashlight to inspect the inside through the last window.

"Goddammit," he muttered as the two contact points of the door alarm came into view. *Paranoid Zorn got them to wire the place.* On the corner of one of the walls was a motion detector. Gerosa saw no wires like the old days, and knew it had to be a cellular network. He returned to the tree line.

"I hope you are up to date with your equipment, Jim. The place is alarmed. It's a cellular network. Has NSA been cooperative in sharing their equipment?"

"They have, but only for use in national security cases, never to come out in court."

"So?"

"So, I'm taking the liberty of declaring this

a national security case, and one of my men just happens to have the device in his black bag." Nelson motioned to one of the agents behind him.

"You are ready to go," he whispered to Gerosa after a few minutes.

"The cellular network for this system has been jammed. Make it quick because the alarm company regularly checks the continuity. If they figure that it is more than a minor blip, they will send someone out here. They don't normally call the local police because it is considered a malfunction on their part, and not a burglary. So we have some time, but not too much."

Gerosa returned to the cabin, opened the door, and motioned the two tech agents to stay outside. He removed the recorder from under the coffee table, and put it in his pocket before motioning them in. They were experienced. Before long, the cars and truck were on their way back to the offsite where it had been confirmed that the reception from the cabin was good.

CHAPTER 25

Meeting at Goldstone office

Annie Larkin barely slept. A day had passed since the time in Gerosa's apartment, and all she could think about was her safety, and the money that would be awaiting her in the Dublin bank. First and foremost was her safety. She finally decided to go with her instincts.

"Michael, we have to speak. Where can we meet?"

Zorn was taken aback by this demand. "Unless there is a problem that could derail our project, there is no reason to meet, particularly not here. I'm going to shut this office down in a few days, and I don't want you to be seen here."

"Give me a time and place, the sooner the better, and yes, there is something that could derail our project."

Zorn thought for a moment. "Meet me in an hour at the Raceway Diner, across from Yonkers Raceway. It's near you. I'll drive up there." He hung up the phone without waiting for a reply, and tried to figure what she was up to. He left the office immediately for Yonkers in his SUV. In the raceway parking lot, he picked a spot that gave him a clear view of the diner across the street, and waited to see her arrive. In the back of his mind was the thought that she might be followed. That was a concern.

Larkin arrived on time. Zorn hesitated to go in as he looked up and down for surveillance. There was none.

Larkin picked a booth to the rear, and as Zorn entered he swept the place looking for anyone who resembled law enforcement, if they were up on her phone, and were already there. This was merely an exercise because he knew the new FBI surveillance unit hired former agents as contractors. Anyone in the diner, regardless of age and male or female, could be an agent. He studied the priest in the corner with an elderly woman for a moment, but realized he could do that with any one of the patrons, and was getting paranoid.

"What's so important and urgent Annie that I have to meet you?" He tried to read her body language as she spoke.

"Michael, there is a little setback, but it should not interfere with our plans. That contractor, Gerosa, is an FBI agent, and he approached me with another agent about you, and what was going on. I played him for a while to see how much he knew, and whether he was just on a fishing expedition. Evidently, something triggered the Bureau to have him hook up with Kieran and me. Whatever it was, they couldn't get anything, or they would have threatened me with arrest, so I told them very little."

Zorn was annoyed that he was unable to figure that out, and the PI he sent down to Florida got bullshitted.

"What exactly did you tell him?" His anger was apparent.

Larkin leaned across the table, and stared at him. "Listen to me, I am going to tell you everything, and what I think is going on. They wanted to know about you and not Burke. I believe that they had info about my past activities with the Agency, probably through an exchange of information. They knew I was living with Burke. With that in mind, they used him to get to me to get me to work for them. They couldn't just approach me without knowing what I was all about, and what I was doing. That was the reason for the dinners, and all the talk.

"I told them I was doing nothing with you as in the past, but you had me looking into gunrunning by the boys on Katonah Avenue, and bringing IRA illegals into the states to raise money, and send it back to Ireland to finance some kind of terrorist activity. I think they bought off on my story. I also told them that I was sick of New York, and would be going back to Ireland. That would cover my departure, albeit in another identity. They wanted me to work for them, but I said no. Probably wanted to beat the Agency to a big case." Larkin waited for a response.

Zorn thought for a moment. *If I shut everything down now, all my work is for naught, and my expectations are all done after Kirkland and Whitaker get through with me. If we continue, Burke will be just a worker who dies at the site. There is no way to connect him to the sarin. Larkin will be gone, and I can decide at the time if I should stay or take my stash of money and start a new life.*

"Annie, let's stay on schedule. There will be nothing to tie Burke into this, and he will be gone."

"What do you mean, he will be missing on his way to Ireland? They will track him down. Then he gives me up, and you have a major Interpol operation to locate me. You are called on the carpet, and put under a microscope."

"Annie, you have worked for the Agency before, and in some hairy situations. You know how we operate when our backs are against the wall. I don't know whether you fell in love with Kieran or not because that is irrelevant. This operation has no room for emotion. The truth is that there is no helicopter to pull Kieran from the mess. He will be dead when the first blast goes off in the elevator shaft. You have to be able to live with that. You are being well compensated."

Zorn considered telling her about the switch to sarin, but decided that it was too much of a risk, and might put her over the top to lay out everything to Gerosa. Larkin was taken back about losing Kieran, but showed no emotion.

"So we go ahead as planned?"

"Let's play it out, and see what happens. We can always abort at the last minute, but for now, we have to be careful. We have the burner phones, but use yours only when necessary. I will do the same. Whenever you go anywhere, clean yourself, and look for any kind of foot surveillance. Look for suspicious cars. Check your apartment every time you enter to see if anyone was in there. You still remember the tricks I taught you, I hope."

Larkin nodded.

"The dynamite is ready to go. Right before nine on the twelfth, I will activate the blasting caps and the altimeters, and that will be it. It is still in the storage facility. Have Kieran bring them in on Sunday the tenth. Monday will be a short day because of the 9/11 commemoration. Tuesday, Kieran will be there bright and early, and will follow the order that you give him on the night before."

"When do I get my identity and plane tickets? And how do I know that I won't be eliminated when everything is in place? Just like Kieran. Why should I trust you?"

Zorn leaned across the table. He spoke softly in what hopefully would be a most convincing manner. "Annie, listen to me. What sense would that make except saving a few dollars for an agency that has a bottomless pit of money. You are not a liability because you will be gone. If anything happens to you, it comes back to bite me. Right now, I may be questioned about you after all is done, and the answer is simple. You were an Agency asset doing some side work for me and Homeland Security by digging up information about gunrunning to Ireland for the New IRA. Nothing came up, and you wanted money that I couldn't pay you, so you returned to Ireland. Let them try to find you under your new identity. To answer your question, on the morning of the twelfth, you will go to Westchester County Airport at 6:00 am, and someone you do not know will approach you and give you everything that you need for a flight to Miami, and then on to Shannon."

Larkin wasn't quite satisfied with the answer he gave about her security. The answers made some sense. She did not mention the recording that Gerosa played for her. Maybe "eliminated" meant her going to Ireland. Not plausible. Whatever, she did not want to disclose that it came from a recorded conversation, assuming that it might lend credibility to her concerns, and possibly accelerate any action against her if it were true. If it was a doctored conversation made specifically to get her to cooperate, then it was irrelevant. Only a few days, and it would be over. She decided to change her routine, and avoid any future meetings. Also, get a room at a local motel until the event was completed.

CHAPTER 26

Sunday Sept 10

Annie Larkin didn't sleep well after engaging in unwanted sex on Sunday morning. She sat on the side of the bed as Burke lay on his back, satisfied.

"Kieran, I've got to stay with a relative at a bed and breakfast on Long Island until our plan is over. We will communicate only when I call you." It came as a surprise to Burke.

"When do we hook up again and where?"

"I have your itinerary and contact info, and will reach out for you a few days after you land in Ireland, and we can start a new life together. One more thing, I want you to avoid Gerosa completely. I don't trust him anymore, and do not need anyone interfering with our plan."

Larkin had been ignoring several phone calls from Gerosa. She let them ring out with no voicemail. She knew that he would be looking for her and Burke.

"Right now, I want you to get moving. Go to the truck rental down the street, and get a small panel truck for the day. Then go to the self-storage. Take the eight tanks down to the site, and store them in the gang box that you set up. You will have to get a hand truck to move them. When you get to the site, park around the corner, so the security guards will not see the truck. Got that?" She tossed him the key to the unit.

"I'll be glad when this is over, and we are together again in Ireland." Burke put on his work clothes, and checked his backpack for his hard hat, reflective vest and protective glasses. The last thing he wanted was to be cited for a safety violation at the site on this day, although the safety people rarely came in on the weekend."

"You nervous?" asked Larkin.

"Fuck no. You don't know half the shit I pulled when I was in Ireland for the New IRA. They loved me because I had balls. No worries here."

"Good, now get moving. This might be the last time I see you for at least a week or two." She pulled him closed and kissed him.

"I'm leaving now, and will call you a few times to make sure everything is in place. Call me only if something is not going as planned. Understand? Sometime early Tuesday, probably around nine, you will get a call. Only two words will be said, 'Do it', and that will be your signal. The helicopter will be on its way waiting to pick you up. Got that?"

Burke nodded, and kissed her again before he left.

After a roundabout trip with Larkin giving directions, and frequently looking for surveillance, she got out of the taxi. It was now Saturday, and she wanted to distance herself from Gerosa and Burke until the twelfth. A block away from the motel, and a short distance from Katonah Avenue, she got out and walked the remaining block.

Often called a "no tell motel" it left to be desired many of the amenities found at a three-star and up, but nonetheless met her needs. Larkin let her sunglasses and floppy brim of her fedora partially cover her face as she scribbled a fictitious name on the registration form. Not that the clerk in the dingy office cared once she produced cash covering an advance deposit for a three-day stay. He barely looked up, and was more concerned about the movie on the outdated television. A small carry-on suitcase that would later facilitate her departure at the airport was her only baggage.

Her room was on the second floor off of a walkway, and a distance from the office. It afforded her privacy. It reeked of stale cigarette smoke, and whether the sheets had been changed was questionable. She decided to sleep on the blanket, and as she laid there, her thoughts about the coming days were in overdrive. Two days before, she put all of her and Burke's non-essential clothing into the local Goodwill box, and left an envelope for the landlady covering the following two weeks' rent.

Burke walked down Katonah Ave towards 233rd St. where a short distance up the hill was a U-Haul lot. The bars weren't open, but he knew he could convince the janitor who was cleaning up the Pipers to open up, and let him have a ball and beer, but he decided that the last thing he needed was to have one of the guards at the site smell alcohol on his breath and report him. He could imbibe as soon as the job was done.

"Give me your license" said the bored clerk at the U-Haul office.

Burke realized that this would leave a paper trail, and reluctantly handed over his dirty NYS license. If Annie had told him this in advance, he would have used a forgery, but what difference would it make at this point?

He found a small panel truck that could meet his needs with tie-down canvass straps in the interior, and handed over cash for a day's rental. The ride to the self-storage was uneventful, and everything was in place. A hand truck was in the corner, which simplified things. In a short time, the eight tanks were loaded into the truck, and secured to the sides with the canvass straps.

Sunday traffic made for a quick trip to the Freedom Tower, and parking on Barclay Street was easy. Burke put on his safety vest over a plain gray sweatshirt rather than his usual Local 18A shirt, and wanted to be as nondescript as possible.

As he rounded the corner towards the Vesey Street entrance pushing the hand truck with three of the eight tanks on it, he tried not to act surprised as he came face to face with Pat Collins, the lather foreman, who was having a smoke.

"What the hell are you doing here on Sunday? Must be ringing the cash register with overtime." was Collins' greeting. Burke hadn't prepared for meeting anyone, particularly someone he knew, so he had to improvise.

"And what the hell are you here for, Pat?" He tried to relax.

"Looking for some overtime also. Have about a dozen men working on sixty, south side, prepping for a pour tomorrow. What's with the tanks?"

"Rizzo with the plumbers asked me to do him a favor, and bring some tanks down. Evidently they were running low, and have a hell of a lot of work to do tomorrow. I want to get into their local someday, and this can't hurt. I've got more talent than to be a laborer all my life. What are you out here for, everybody smokes on site on the weekends? You didn't see any safety people, did you?"

"Why, you want to grab a nip with me over at Lillie's. They are doing breakfast for the tourists, but will pour a shot or two in the backroom. With all the money we spend there, they can't afford not to."

"I'll pass for now. Might see you there later though." Burke walked away pushing the tanks, not wanting to converse further. On the way to the Vesey Street gate, he noticed that sweat was coming through the armpits of his sweatshirt. He decided that the remainder of the tanks would be brought in at the other two entrances, and hoped he could catch the hoist operators at their change of shift, so he would not be seen twice by the same person.

It was easier than he anticipated. The bored security guard barely looked at him to match the picture on his swipe card with his face, and the handheld scanning device lit up green, verifying his identity. Once in, the hoist operator barely noticed him as the reading of the New York Post, and latest rock music coming through earpieces took precedence. The outdoor hoist rattled up fifty-nine floors as Burke admired the New York landscape on this cloud free day. He couldn't help thinking that in a few days this view would be no more.

On floor fifty-nine he thanked the operator who couldn't care less, and wheeled the tanks out towards the stairwell. He carried the tanks up to the sixtieth floor not wanting to leave a trail. Then to the gang box that he had placed near the elevator shafts. This will be easy, he thought as he paused at one of the elevator banks on the east side of the building. He didn't know why he was told by Annie to use that particular shaft; probably because its proximity to the entrance to the Port Authority Transit Hub or PATH as it was commonly known. Thousands of commuters use the transit system as they go to and from New Jersey.

The gang box lay undisturbed just where Burke had placed it after taking it from one of the other trades that abandoned it after leaving the site. It was old and rusty, but met his needs, and accommodated the eight tanks. It was placed close enough to the elevator bank where he could accomplish his mission in the minimum amount of time.

Burke returned the U-Haul, and walked briskly to the Piper's, which was now open.

"Jimmy, give me a Guinness and a shot of Jameson's," he said to the bartender who was setting the four flat screen televisions to cover the day's Irish football and soccer games being beamed across the ocean. The smell of stale beer lingered, and the bar was beginning to fill up, many of the patrons having attended the noon mass at St. Barnabas nearby on 241st Street. Pipers served a genuine Irish breakfast in addition to the bar sales.

Burke was pleased with himself, and anticipated Tuesday with a sense of accomplishment. Shit, his name will go down in history with the best of the IRA. He downed his Jameson's in one gulp, and as he enjoyed the smooth flow of the Guinness washing it down, he felt a tap on his shoulder.

"Top of the morning," said Gerosa sarcastically. "Coming from the noon mass?"

"No no. How are you Dickie?" said a surprised Burke. "What are ya havin'?" asked Burke as he slid a twenty across the bar.

"Lookin' for Annie." Gerosa did not introduce Michaels who was standing behind him. "Nothing for us, a little too early. Where is she, I have to talk to her. Got her a nice job in the city, but she has to report there early tomorrow, and I have to get in touch with her."

"I'll be honest with ya, she took off today for a few days. Said she was staying with some relative at some bed and breakfast on the island. Give her a call."

"Tried that, Kieran, but only got a ring off. Why don't you try?"

Something didn't sound right to Burke, but he took out his flip-top phone, and tried to call Larkin. He also got a ring off.

"Nothing lads, maybe she is at mass, and left the phone at the bed and breakfast."

Gerosa thought about breaking his cover, drag Burke outside, and threaten the shit out of him, but realized that up to this point he had no case, and if nothing came out of it, he would be the fall guy for everything that had gone on up to this point. He decided to let it go.

"If you hear from her, have her call me. This is a good job opportunity."

Gerosa walked down Katonah Avenue and got into his truck. "What do you make of it, Eddie?" he asked Michaels who got into the passenger seat.

"He's either a good bullshitter or he's telling the truth. I don't know what to make of it. If we knew he was going to call her, and be on the line, we could get the phone company to triangulate the call, and get us a location, but that is a major task rarely done except in national security investigations."

"Well, what is this?"

Michaels stopped and shook his head. "Don't you realize how deep we are in this right now? If we can't find out what they are all up to, and the real connect with Zorn, we'll probably end up in jail."

"What about surveillance?"

Michaels shook his head. "Can't get the personnel unless we lay out everything, and then too many questions will be asked. Should have had a Jameson's back there, this is all giving me a headache."

CHAPTER 27

FBI Office

"I like to believe you guys, and extended

myself to my own detriment in this case. Tell me something good is happening or is going to happen." Rick Dean leaned back in the leather swivel chair behind his desk, his hands clasped on his lap waiting for an update.

Michaels and Gerosa looked at each other, hoping the other would speak first. It was not to be a fun meeting.

"We're still waiting," Michaels started, "The microphone in the cabin is dead. No one has been there since it was installed. We're hoping we get something tomorrow. Zorn's GPS tracking device shows no unusual movement."

Dean leaned forward and put his elbows on his desk. Not a man to show anxiety easily, his demeanor showed that he was now visibly bothered. "What are you trying to tell me, that we have reached a dead end with one day to go?"

Michaels interjected, "We still have two days to go on the court order, but my bet is that something will happen tomorrow."

"Do we know where the judge and Whitaker will be tomorrow, or are we to assume that they will be in the cabin?"

"We have an idea where the judge will be," said Michaels. "I called his chambers on a pretext, and they said that he will be at the commemoration ceremony tomorrow down at the 9/11 memorial, along with several city and state officials."

"That kind of negates any kind of terrorism or whatever is happening down there. The judge wouldn't be planning something, and then be in the middle of it when it goes down, and become another statistic. Besides, that area will be as secure as Fort Knox with all the dignitaries in attendance. Doesn't make sense."

"Maybe it's just a distraction, and he won't be there at all," said Michaels.

"What about Whitaker and Zorn?" countered Dean."

"No idea," was the response from Gerosa who had been silent up to this point. "We couldn't get a surveillance team on them for sake of blowing the whole operation if they got made. Besides, Zorn was with the Agency, and would be alert for surveillance should anything heavy be going on."

"My last question," said Dean, "What is the story with your new informant that you supposedly turned, Annie Larkin? Or was it the other way around? You didn't come in blowing your horn about what she has been telling you, so I assume you got nothing. Correct?"

"She's in the wind," answered Michaels, "but we are trying to get to her."

"Fucking great," said Dean, who rarely used profanity. "Well, you've dug yourself a hole, and the only thing we can do is pray something comes up before the court order runs out. And if that happens, we are all in deep shit, or I should say I am. Dick, you can go back to your retired lifestyle, Eddie, you can put your papers in, and I'm stuck here with a year to go until retirement, and will probably get fired. We'll regroup tomorrow."

CHAPTER 28

Freedom Tower construction site, 9/11

"Where the hell have you been?" Eddie Michaels didn't have to look at the caller ID. The Irish brogue told him it was Willie O'Shea. It was 8:00 am, he had been up since five, and already made two calls to Gerosa in the hope something had come up. He also called the monitoring location, and learned there was no activity in the cabin.

"Good morning, Willie, what's up?"

"You haven't been down here lately, and I've got to talk to you. Can you come down here this morning?"

"Willie, I've got a lot of shit going on, and besides, that whole area will be packed with the ceremony going on. Can't do it Willie."

"Now Eddie, listen to this old Irishman. Get your ass down here. I have something that might be important to you. You've been calling me once a week asking me about Kieran Burke, who I told you about, and every time I ask you what is going on, you tell me nothing. Well, a bullshitter can tell a bullshitter, and you are one. I told you something was fishy with that guy, and old Willie was on the money. Something happened yesterday that I got to talk to you about. Take the subway down here, and I'll meet you at Lilly O'Brien's in the basement, where we can have a pint. What time can you be here?"

Michaels didn't want to waste his time, but Burke's name got his attention.

"Willie, I can be there in an hour or so. Isn't it a little early for a beer, and aren't you supposed to lay off the alcohol when you're going back to the site. You know, I can report you," he said kiddingly.

"Eddie, many of the construction guys have a liquid breakfast here. Of course they are from other sites, not the Freedom Tower." A brief chuckle followed. "A little hair of the dog on those tough mornings. They come and go through the back entrance so as not to be seen. As for me, I probably won't go back to work. The place will clear out before the ceremony ends, and unless some donkey hurts himself before then, I won't be going back. You know I'm the shop steward, and have to handle accident reports."

Willie laughed between coughs, and Michaels assumed he was starting to go through his morning pack of Marlboros.

"I'll see you at nine," said Michaels as his adrenaline started pumping. Maybe this might be a break he was looking for. After hanging up, he dialed Gerosa's cell phone, and told him what was happening. Gerosa wanted to go with, but Michaels waved him off, telling him there was always the possibility that Burke could come in and recognize him.

Michaels arrived on schedule, and went to the basement of the pub where a group of construction workers were having breakfast, some liquid. A lot of work-related chatter filled the air while a waitress hustled about, knowing that tips were good with this group. O'Shea was in a corner booth with a pint of Guinness, and was counseling a young worker who he promptly dismissed when he saw Michaels.

"Willie, what's going on?"

"No, you tell me. You came down here pretty quickly, so you must have something going."

"Willie, you know I can't discuss what is going on, but if this turns out the way I hope it will, I'll get you some kind of Medal of Freedom or maybe a case of Jameson's."

"Give me a case of Jameson's, and you can take a bottle out for yourself." Another gruff laugh.

The waitress quickly arrived and took their order, Michaels content with coffee, and O'Shea a full Irish breakfast of bacon eggs, black pudding and bread. He looked at Michaels. "There is an old saying, 'Eat breakfast like a King, lunch like a prince, and dine like a pauper.'"

"You forgot that your arteries will be clogged

before you leave the table."

O'Shea ignored the comment. "Here's what I think you might be interested in. It's a good thing I came in today because Pat Collins, the lather foreman, comes into my shanty. Usually, he sends one of his men to pick up supplies that we give out, such as protective equipment, small tools, and whatever the carpenters, lathers and laborers need. This time he personally came in. The concrete contractor, Cosentino Construction, pays for it all under the time and material contract so we give it out freely. Which reminds me, you need any rain gear or work gloves? I have plenty, and can give you some the next time I see you."

"Now Willie, are you attempting to bribe a federal agent?"

"Hell no, I just want you to have the proper clothing when the weather gets rainy down here, and when you have to go up and down the ladders."

"Okay, let's get to the point. What did Collins have to say?"

"Well, greedy bastard that he is, he was here yesterday to get some overtime although, in fairness, he had some people working. He tells me that he ran into Kieran around noon pushing a handcart with three acetylene tanks on it. That is nothing that he would normally be doing, so he says he was doing a favor for the plumber foreman. So, I do some investigating. I went to Andy Rizzo, the plumber, and he knows nothing about acetylene. Says they have plenty. So that gets my Irish curiosity going even more, and I check with the hoist operator who happened to be here yesterday as well. He says that one of the laborers made three trips up, and he wasn't sure of the floor, but believes that it was the fifty-ninth. Wasn't sure if it was Burke because he was reading the paper, but sure as hell sounds like it was him. Nothing was said between them." O'Shea leaned back in his chair. "So, what do you think?"

A surge of excitement shot through Michaels. He looked at his watch, and saw that the 9/11 ceremony with the reading of the 3,000 names was already underway. Michaels wanted to be in a position to respond to an anticipated terrorist act, which he believed was imminent, but he decided to meet O'Shea. He received no phone calls, and heard no disruption of the ceremony. The pause in the reading of the victims' names at 8:46 am when American Airlines flight 11 hit floors 93 to 99 on the north tower, and at 9:03 am when United flight 175 hit the south tower went by without incident.

O'Shea's information about Burke gave rise to the secondary theory that whatever was going to occur would be the day after 9/11, a day when all the security would be gone, but a day that would have impact because of the heavy commuter traffic, and full workforce.

The waitress delivered a plate of sizzling meat and eggs, emitting the smell of burning butter.

"Willie, I got to go. You just told me something that could be important. Keep your phone on, and hang around here all day. How can I get some agents down here later today, without alerting anyone, to search for where those acetylene tanks went?"

"That's easy Eddie." O'Shea dug into his worn wallet, filled with a pile of business cards, and pulled out three. "These are Local 18A cards that we use for visitors from the outside that don't have a business card; a requirement that is needed to get a day pass. Have someone type in the names of whoever is coming down, and have their driver's license ID ready to show. By all means, don't show a badge or credentials." O'Shea winked.

"Have them give me a call, and I will come and get them as they have to have an escort. I'll take them around, and they can do whatever they want, and if they want some tools, I can get them. No one will know what is going on except me."

O'Shea had a Cheshire cat smile when Michaels excused himself, and went back to the office with the reading of the victims' names barely audible as he walked to the subway.

CHAPTER 29

New York FBI Office

Michaels went directly to Dean's Office after leaving O'Shea. On the way he called Gerosa to join him.

They met in the lobby. Gerosa knew that something was going on by the smile on Michaels' face, and his hurry to get to Dean's office. "Wait until we get there," he told an inquisitive Gerosa.

They burst into Dean's office bypassing Susan, his secretary, whose looks could have killed. Dean was pacing about nervously waiting for a phone call from the monitoring location that something had come over the wire putting Kirkland and Whitaker into something illegal, and in the end game, saving his ass from perhaps getting fired.

"Tell me something good," he said to Michaels as he sat at his coffee table rather than his bureaucratic position behind his mahogany desk. Michaels and Gerosa sat across from him. Michaels recounted O'Shea's story, which brought an air of excitement to the trio.

"What do you need to go forward?" asked Dean.

"First, I need two agents to get down to the site around 3:00 pm when almost all the workers will be gone to meet with O'Shea, and start looking for the tanks," Michaels started. He gave the names of two agents that he worked with previously on the Drug Task Force, and Dean nodded approval.

"Second, I want you to have a crew come up from the laboratory tonight. Have them drive up in the evidence recovery truck that can check and test for everything imaginable, and have them stand by should something develop, which I think might happen. What would Burke be doing bringing possibly acetylene tanks to the site, and giving a bullshit story why he was there?"

"Why don't we pick him up? Try to turn him?" asked Dean.

"No, he's too hard core," answered Michaels. "Remember, he has the IRA in his background. Trying to turn him is too risky. We want to get Whitaker and Kirkland in the loop. We know they are somehow involved, and it appears they have motives. Also, suppose the tanks are legit, for some company on the site. Maybe Burke didn't want to tell the lather foreman what he was doing. Maybe getting some cash for doing someone a favor."

"It's too coincidental." said Gerosa.

Before continuing, Michaels excused himself to take a call from his cell phone. Dean and Gerosa heard only the one side of the conversation, which was only a "Yes, great, what time, good, thanks a million, keep me informed, I owe you."

"Bingo," said Michaels. "Whitaker and Kirkland will be going to the cabin tonight, and will be there through tomorrow."

Michaels saw the puzzled looks on Dean's and Gerosa's faces, and returned them with a big smile.

"Things look like they may be falling into place. The person on the other end of the call told me that Kirkland and Whitaker are going to the cabin tonight. They are to meet at the helicopter service at Westchester County Airport at 8:00 pm to go to the cabin. I asked the County Police to monitor all flight plans daily, and check for any going upstate with the name Whitaker on it. Didn't want to mention Kirkland because it might raise someone up."

"That's good so far, but what's the guarantee that we can get them talking about anything that might or might not happen at the site? Say we find the tanks, and something is amiss with them, which I'm sure there is. My guess they are filled with dynamite, which from my knowledge would do little damage to the site. Say all that happens, and we arrest Burke. What then? Whitaker and Kirkland are waiting for some kind of news that whatever they were planning happened, which is not coming. Suppose they have no discussion or something vague. Then we have only Burke. We can't find Larkin, and we can't implicate Zorn. So what do we have? A dead wire? What happens when Kirkland and Whitaker receive notices three months from now? No one in their right mind, particularly Siano, would dare drag them before a grand jury. So now what?"

Michaels and Gerosa saw the problem. Michaels broke the few moments of silence. "I have an idea, but I have to work out the details. Rick, can you have a SWAT team in the vicinity of the cabin tomorrow to make arrests?"

"Are you fuckin' nuts? If this pans out, it will be hard enough to bring all this to a grand jury, and get indictments, and keep out your activities with the mike. A SWAT team is out of the question. They need a full background of the case, the individuals involved. They have to come up with a plan that has to be approved up the line. Can you imagine the stir this will cause in this office, if this case gets out at this point? Take one step at a time, and if we get what we want, it will go to a grand jury. That's it."

"What about flight?" asked Gerosa. This guy Whitaker has contacts overseas, and could be gone in a heartbeat if he gets a subpoena. And Kirkland. He is connected all the way up to the top in the Justice Department, and no matter what is said, it could be twisted to look like innocent observations. Once that happens, they stop looking for Whitaker, and he comes back, and continues to run his business."

Dean got up, which was a signal that the

meeting was over. "Let's let this play out. And Eddie, whatever you have up your sleeve, keep me advised no matter what time of night it is."

CHAPTER 30

Bronx, NY

The ceiling of the drab motel room was no different from the walls; white that had turned a light brown from years of cigarette smoke and an inattentive management. Annie Larkin was on the bed staring at a moaning ceiling fan, its blades crusted with dust. She was weighing her options in what was going to happen in the next sixteen hours, and how she could best protect herself.

Was the money really going to be where Zorn said it would be? He could show her proof in a text or email before she got on the plane to Ireland, but who's to say the email wasn't fabricated or, if valid, the money wasn't transferred back after she was on the plane. Was she in too deep at this point? That Goddamn Gerosa was an agent, and a pretty good one to fool her. He now knows she is up to something, and what happens if everything goes as scheduled tomorrow. It's six hours to Ireland, and a lot can happen in that amount of time. They could catch

Burke, and he rolls on her, and the next thing there is a picture of her at the airport. A false identity that Zorn promised would not cover her if the Garda or Interpol had a picture, and flooded the customs agents at the airport with it. And worst of all, suppose that the tape that they played for her was real, and Zorn, in fact, planned to kill her. He was capable, and from what he told her about the Agency, it could be done easily without a trace.

She went into the bathroom, reluctant to use it, but looked at herself in the mirror. *Getting older,* she thought, but still have a few miles left if I don't act stupid. She made her decision to survive as best she could, and called a car service.

"Eddie, I'm going home to get some sleep. Was going to wait it out with you here, but I need some rest." said Gerosa. He and Michaels were in the special operations location, an office building in an industrial park in New Jersey, monitoring what was transpiring at the cabin and at the site.

"I'll let you know if anything happens," Michaels said. Kirkland and Whitaker are due to arrive at the cabin around 8:45 pm, and O'Shea met the two agents at the site. They began their search, but there was no determining how long it would take to find the tanks if O'Shea was on the money. The lab vehicle is on its way if we need them, but is hung up in traffic in the Beltway."

The only loose end was what Michaels thought could be a hare-brained scheme with the tech section in special operations, and a contact he had in the private sector. That would take about five hours.

"Tomorrow will be a long day, and I need a shower and change of clothes," said Gerosa as he walked out the door.

He made good time driving to the Bronx, and pulled his truck into his parking space where he fidgeted with his key ring. Finding the key to his first floor apartment, he entered, and flipped on the hall light. Seeing a figure on the living room couch, he dove to the floor, and pulled out his 9 mm P224 SIG Sauer. Rolling once, he ended in a prone position, his pistol aimed center mass at the silhouette.

"Relax Dick, it is only me."

It finally registered. Annie Larkin was sitting on his couch, as calm as could be. Gerosa rose slowly from the floor, his pistol still pointed at Larkin.

"What the fuck are you doing here? I could have shot you." Larkin put on the end table light, and Gerosa saw that she was only armed with a slight smile.

"How'd you get in here?"

Larkin reached into her small pocketbook, and pulled out a black packet containing lock picking rakes and tension tools. "You forgot that I have been around for a while overseas, where I learned a lot. Now, I understand that you have been looking for me. Well, here I am."

Gerosa knew that it had to be something more than chitchat or some negative information about Zorn that would cause her to come to his apartment in person, and gain entry the way that she did. He replaced the pistol in his ankle holster.

"Let's cut to the chase, Annie. I don't have time to waste with bullshit stories. You came here to see me. For what?"

"I want my 'get out of jail card' that you referred to when you first told me who you really were. Good job, by the way. I'm usually good at seeing through people."

"That's a figure of speech meaning that you tell me everything that you know that you are involved in, and in return, if it pans out, I keep you out of jail by speaking to the U. S. Attorney who is handling the case. Got the picture?"

"That's what I thought, just wanted to hear you say it, but what guarantees do I have?"

Gerosa was a little surprised. This hard nosed former, or possibly still CIA asset, now wanted to cooperate.

"The only guarantee is my word, and that is better than any piece of paper that I could give you."

Larkin arose from the couch and paced about. "Okay, let's talk. But if I get fucked in this deal……" She stopped mid-sentence.

"You will do what," said Gerosa. "You don't have any high cards in this game, and if you want to walk out of here right now, nothing changes.

But if you are with me, you are with me one hundred percent. One lie or double cross, and all bets are off, and you will be prosecuted along with whomever is involved in whatever is going on. You understand?"

Larkin sat back down, and began her story, emphasizing that she was acting in good conscience believing that she was working for the CIA under the direction of Zorn. All she knew was that something was going to take place at the Freedom Tower, and involved dynamite that was to be set off by Burke. She knew nothing about anyone named Kirkland or Whitaker, and believed everything she was doing was in the long run for God and Country.

Gerosa listened for about an hour not taking any notes. He noticed that Larkin had the small suitcase that she was going to travel with.

"Put that in the bedroom. You will stay here tonight. I will sleep on the couch. Don't leave here, no matter what you hear or see. Can you contact Zorn now?"

"I can try, but when we left off, I was supposed to contact him early tomorrow to find out where to pick up my new identity and bank information in Ireland. I think calling him now might spook him."

Gerosa agreed, and used his cell phone to reach Michaels. "Eddie, patch us through to Rick. He has to be in on what I want to tell you." A few phone beeps and Dean was on the line. Gerosa repeated what Larkin had told him.

"Nothing about Kirkland and Whitaker, the important players in this scheme" Dean noted somewhat annoyed. "We are still missing the most important part of this case."

Michaels updated Dean and Gerosa on what was transpiring at the site. "Our guys are down there with O'Shea, but have found nothing yet. They checked floor 59, and are starting on 60 now. There are so many shanties, locked areas, and tanks already locked up in their safety cages that this is going to be a monumental undertaking. If we go gangbusters, and rip everything apart, word will get out quickly. The whole thing will be blown. I guess the question is how far we want to play this out. Take out Burke now, and who can he give us if he wanted to? Remember he is hard core. If he did, at best we would get Larkin, who is now in our camp. He has been insulated from Zorn and the others."

Dean knew that they were waiting for some direction. "Let's play it this way. If we can't find any tanks, we'll just have to see what Burke does in the morning. Can your guys pick him up as he comes in for work? Do we need more manpower down there?"

"I can work things out," said Michaels "But it will not be easy. There are a lot of people working there. The hoists are jammed in the morning, there is a crowd of workers, and sometimes there is a line waiting to go up, so we could lose him even if we pick him up at the gate. Or, if he is really cute, he could get off on one floor, and race up or down a stairwell, and exit another floor. In other words, he can dry clean himself.

"We are not sure where the tanks are hidden, but presume they are on the upper floors in some way will be tossed down the elevator shaft. Anything can happen there in the morning. He could arrive, we lose him, and then he goes where we are not expecting him to be, and he does what he has to do before we get to stop him. Then we have a real problem. The two guys down there are good, and if you send more they will get lost, and be useless. Sure you want to play it this way, Rick? This could literally blow up in our faces."

"Keep it the way I said for now. If there is any change, I will let you know immediately,"

"What's going on at the cabin?"

"No smoking gun," said Dean, "Only small talk about something going to happen tomorrow. They seem to be in a good mood, but are a little concerned about Zorn. I don't think they totally trust him. No specifics on what is going to happen tomorrow. Damn."

"Can't talk about it now, Rick. I am working on something that might tickle the wire a little bit. Get something incriminating," said Michaels. Dean didn't pursue the comment because from experience it could be something that he didn't want to hear.

"What about Zorn? Where is he?" asked

Michaels.

"The GPS shows he is at home in Scarsdale. No indication there is anyone with him except his wife. Kind of a loner socially."

"Get some sleep, and we will regroup tomorrow," said Dean before he terminated the call.

"Okay Annie. What is your schedule tomorrow?"

"I'm supposed to meet someone tomorrow at a place near Westchester County Airport, and get my ID and plane tickets and a thousand dollars in cash to carry me over until I can get to the bank in Ireland. I'll get a call at six thirty with the location for the meeting, and I am to go directly there, and wait for someone acting on Zorn's behalf. Then I'm on the nine o'clock flight to Fort Lauderdale. From there an evening flight to Shannon Airport."

"Do you think that the recording that I played for you was doctored to scare you, and get you to cooperate? I'll tell you now that was no bullshit or a fake recording. I'm going to stick with you tomorrow, and see what happens. You good with that?"

"After what you just said, I can only believe you. Will be glad to have you backing me up."

"Okay, get some sleep. I'll be up early to shower, and wake you when I'm done. Clean towels are on the shelf in the bathroom. I'll be on the couch if you need me, but be aware I sleep with my gun." Gerosa smiled before he took a blanket and pillow out of the hall closet.

CHAPTER 31

Cabin in Wyndham, NY

The helicopter arrived as scheduled, blowing loose dirt around the makeshift landing area. Kirkland and Whitaker deplaned after a wave to the pilot. Kirkland entered the cabin first, shut off the alarm system, and turned on the gas fireplace.

"Ready for a drink?" he asked Whitaker as he made his way to the liquor cabinet. Not waiting for a response, he poured two glasses of Maker's Mark bourbon.

"What do you think?" he asked Whitaker, who was silent. "You look concerned."

"There have been a lot of changes mid-stream with Michael. I hope he is up to the task."

Kirkland handed Whitaker one of the glasses, and raised it as making a toast. "He has been okay so far. I trust him to get things done. Well, we will know tomorrow, won't we? My only concern is there enough layers of insulation between us and him. Let's catch what Fox News has to say."

Kirkland picked up the remote, and aimed it at the flat screen mounted above the fireplace. The remainder of the evening was spent in small talk until the eleven o'clock news was over. The two conspirators bid their good nights, and went to their respective bedrooms.

"God damn it." The agent at the monitoring station took off his headset. He looked at his partner. "Nothing. They've been there for over two hours. Haven't said shit. Who's Michael?"

"Damned if I know. I was told very little about this case when Dean sent me over here. All I have is a list of keywords here, which if I hear mentioned, I am to turn on the recorder. And to use a lot of leeway if I think they are talking about a third party. Now we wait until tomorrow."

CHAPTER 32

Morning of Sept 12

Gerosa hardly slept, and arose before five. He peeked in at Larkin.

"Good morning Dick." She was on her back with the covers pulled up to her neck. "Couldn't sleep much last night. Been through many things in my life, but I always knew where I was going the day before. Last night wasn't like that. It's no different this morning."

"Well, join the club. I couldn't sleep also. Million things going on in my mind. No definite answers. Don't have much here for breakfast, but will put some coffee on." Larkin smiled and nodded.

Gerosa moved to the kitchen, content that she didn't bail out on him through the bedroom window. While the coffee was brewing, he called Michaels.

"Eddie, anything new?"

"No, they have been down there all night. I

haven't checked in the last few hours, but I presume they will call me if they come up with anything. Where is Larkin?"

"I had her stay here for the night and I'm making coffee now. Then, I'm going to take her to meet Zorn or his representative supposedly to get her new ID, and some cash as soon as she gets a call as to the time and location. I don't believe it's going to go down that way, so I will cover her."

"Did Zorn ever see you before?"

"No, aside from the PI he sent to Florida to get info on me, he doesn't know what I look like, so it should be cool."

"Dick, as a further backup, I'm sending Tom English over to your apartment in an undercover car."

"Make it one of those Town Cars like a limo service. That is what she would normally use as transportation. And make sure it has livery cab plates."

"Will do, Dick, I really don't want Zorn or one of his operatives seeing you. He's pretty slick, so don't assume anything or underestimate him. Our analyst has been going over the phone records for his cell phone, home, and the CIA office, and it appears that he has been in contact with some interesting characters. One call in particular went to a security company run by a couple of former CIA black ops guys. Their reputation is that they will do anything for money, and I wouldn't put it past Zorn to use them for his dirty work. Be careful?

"Okay Eddie, keep me advised as to what is going on."

The call came early at 6:15. Larkin was on her second cup of coffee as she looked at her cell phone. "Burner phone," she said to Gerosa as she flipped the lid and took the call. All that was said was "Go to the Holiday Inn off 684 near the airport by 8:30, and wait for a call," before the hang-up. Larkin thought it sounded like Zorn, but wasn't sure.

Tom English arrived in a late model Lincoln Town Car a little after 7:30, and tapped his horn lightly in front of Gerosa's apartment. He had on a black suit, white shirt, and black tie. Moments later, Gerosa and Larkin were heading for the Holiday Inn.

"Tommy, where are you going after this? To LaGuardia to try to get a fare? All you need is a black cap." Gerosa wanted to lighten up what could be a tense situation.

"What's up?" said English, ignoring the remark. "All I got from Eddie was that this was a rush job, and I was to come here, and pick you up to cover your ass just like we did in the old days when you were buying a kilo of heroin." He looked at Larkin through the rearview mirror. "I'm Tom English, here to serve and protect."

Gerosa cut him off, and his kidding tone changed. "Tom, this is Annie, and this isn't just a bodyguard detail. Serious shit, so take it seriously."

Gerosa laid out a little of the background of the case, emphasizing that Larkin's life could be in danger in that she was to pick up a substantial sum of money and a new ID at the motel. The next move was for her to be called as to where at the hotel she should meet to make the transaction. A quarter mile from the motel parking lot, Gerosa got out.

"I'll walk from here. Keep your phone on, so I know what's happening."

"10-4 Dick. His Bluetooth earpiece did not look suspicious, and fit in with what a limo driver would be wearing. Gerosa had a similar earpiece so his hands would be free.

The limo pulled into the parking lot, a short distance from the manager's office. The call came at 8:15, and Larkin answered after one ring. She had already been coached by English and Gerosa on how to act.

"Meet me in room 203," was all that was said.

Larkin knew it was not Zorn on the other end. Loud enough to be picked up on English's earpiece, she answered. "No, I'll meet you in the breakfast area, and we can have coffee while I check the goods."

"I said the room. Do it." was the response.

Larkin had been told how to respond, but she didn't have to act much. She had been in difficult situations before.

"Listen, I don't know who the fuck you are. I was promised something, and I want it on my conditions. Right now. Or everything up to this point goes down the shitter. You got that?"

There was a pause on the other end of the line. Zorn's operative from the same rogue security agency that he used to get the sarin gas was on the other end of the line. He had an envelope full of blank papers. His orders were for him to lure her to the room and kill her. Now he had to change midstream. Just a minor change, he thought, a possibility he anticipated. His car, which he didn't register when he checked in the previous night, was parked where he could make a quick exit to the Interstate.

"What do you want to do, sweetheart?" he said sarcastically with a hint of anger. "If that is you in the limo that I see out front, pull around to the rear of the motel, and I will come down, and we can meet in the car."

The operative wanted the limo near his car, so he could make a quick exit. *Shame that the poor bastard trying to make a living has to go too, but there is no other choice,* he thought.

"Done," said Larkin, who now believed that she was being set up.

"Be careful Tom. This is all bullshit. Something's not right, and I'm not armed."

"That's all right, I am," said English as he patted the Glock in his shoulder holster. "When you see him coming, get out of the car, and go to him. He won't do anything out in the open, and if I see anything going wrong, I'm going to take him down."

Gerosa and English went over their plan after the hang-up of Larkin's call.

Within minutes, a well-built man in his early thirties wearing a black suit and raincoat came around the rear walkway surrounding the hotel. He could easily have blended in with the several pilots from the nearby airport who regularly stayed there. Larkin got out of the back seat, and started to approach him. The operative saw what she was doing, and moved quickly towards her, pulling a small .22 caliber automatic from his raincoat pocket. Partially covering it with his palm, he pulled Larkin close as giving her a greeting hug.

"Get the fuck back into the car."

Larkin did not have time to react or think about her next move as she backpedaled to the back seat. English now had his Glock out pointed at them, but her back blocked his target. As she opened the rear door, operative's pistol moved to her head.

"Drop the gun into the back seat," he said to English, "and no one gets hurt." He lied, and English knew it, but he had no alternative. He slowly did as he was told.

"Now drive over next to that Lexus you see parked in the back, and...." The operative stopped mid-sentence as he felt the cold steel of a pistol against the back of his head.

"Drop the gun. It's over." Gerosa was reaching

through the open rear window. Operative let the gun drop as he saw no alternative. Gerosa slowly opened the car door, withdrew his hand from the open window when the operative pushed his full weight against the door, slamming Gerosa to the ground. He reached back into the car fumbling for the gun he dropped on the rear seat. Then his lights went out.

"God damn, you're good." English said as he was looking over the seat at Larkin who had his gun in her hand, the butt of which had a small blood stain from where she clocked the operative before he could grab his gun.

"I'll second that," followed Gerosa as he pushed away the operative who had landed on him as he fell backwards out the door.

"Cuff him and put him in the back with me. Annie can ride up front with you. Call the County Police, and see if they can escort us to the city line. We can pick up a PD unit there to get us back to the office quickly. I'll call our White Plains office, have someone pick up this guy's car, and interview the manager to see what he put on his registration form."

The drive was uneventful with the operative refusing to answer any questions. Gerosa went through his wallet. He found some interesting cards. One, in particular, was Michael Zorn's Homeland Security card.

"Can't you do this in front, and loosen it a little? I have no circulation in my hands?" The operative complained about the plastic flex cuffs that bound his wrists tightly behind his back.

Gerosa looked at him deadpanned. "Fuck you."

CHAPTER 33

September 12

"This is where it all comes together," said Whitaker as he was watching a Keurig machine drain coffee into his cup in the small kitchen adjacent to the living room. Whitaker had a glimpse of the flat screen television mounted above the gas-fed fireplace, one of the luxuries Kirkland permitted in the old stone cabin. The helicopter pilot was directed to pick them up later in the day, but they anticipated that all air traffic would be halted at that time.

Kirkland was up earlier, and was fixated on Fox News, the only channel he watched, now playing on the flatscreen.

"Did you hear from Zorn?" he asked.

"No, but he is reliable, and I assume he took care of the female's situation one way or another."

"What about launching the main player?"

Whitaker checked the time on the television. "It is 8:35 now, so we will know in twenty-five minutes."

Assistant United States Attorney Siano was in the offsite tech room with the two FBI agents. He wanted to make sure that whatever was recorded was done in accordance with the law regarding the monitoring of conversations.

"Goddamn! Close, but we still don't have a case," said Siano, "They could easily explain that conversation as being innocuous. We need something better."

The agents were frustrated. They came in at midnight for a twelve-hour shift, and were weary of the inactivity. The wire was silent except for the background chatter on the Fox News channel.

It was now 9:05, and the rush of commuters arriving at the PATH station next to the Tower was at its height, looking like a swarm of ants from the 60th floor. All the tower workers were busy plying their respective trades, oblivious to their surroundings.

Whitaker and Kirkland were impatient as the clock reached 9:10, but the break in the regular programming came at 9:22.

"Breaking News," flashed on the screen, and the program shifted to a reporter for special events, Geoff Young, who was in a makeshift studio.

"Ladies and Gentlemen," he began, "we have a major event unfolding at Tower 1, the Freedom Tower, which as you know is still under construction, and is presently up to the 65th floor. I am two blocks away from the site, and have been told to evacuate our small studio here, but I want to get the facts out before I go. From what I have been told by police sources rushing to the scene, there has been some kind of attack on the tower involving poison gas. Police have been told to avoid the area, although several have responded and have fallen on the street. There is complete chaos. We are trying to get our helicopter into position to get some aerial views, but they have been told to stay away."

"Son of a bitch," said Whitaker, "We got it done. I wasn't sure how well Zorn would perform, but he got it done. The switch from dynamite to gas was brilliant."

Young continued his reporting. "I apologize to the viewers for not having video at the scene, but law enforcement won't permit it." Sirens wailed in the background.

"Ambulances are attempting to rush to the scene, but are being held back if they do not have the proper protective equipment. I repeat, there appears to be complete chaos going on. I just received an update from a high-level FBI source that says they have documentation showing that there were threats of some kind of terrorist act at the tower from Al-Qaeda, and the intelligence experts believe that this is the result of the threats. It appears that once again, the dots were not connected, or law enforcement got lazy."

"Perfect" said Kirkland. "We have everything

we wanted. Now it is up to the president and Congress to act. I have garnered enough support of legal scholars to back the legality of an immediate strike against several of our enemy countries to put an end to terrorism once and for all."

"I have had my lobbyists working on congress for a while now ensuring a vote for war should any terrorism related catastrophe happen," said Whitaker, "I know it is early, but I can use a drink to celebrate that we are the ones who ultimately will be responsible for the elimination of terrorism in the world. If the public only knew, we would be heroes."

"I have always believed that the end justifies the means, and that is the case here," said Kirkland. By the way, where is Zorn?"

"I didn't want him to contact us after this went down. There is no reason to. When all the dust settles, or I should say gas," Whitaker smiled, "He will be rewarded handsomely."

Their attention again focused on the television, where Young continued his reporting.

AUSA Siano smiled as he watched the agents record Whitaker and Kirkland's conversation. He had his own headset and gave a thumbs up when they looked at him for a sign of approval. He had been jotting down notes from the overheard conversation.

"I'm going to leave you gentlemen here to finish up. I'm going downtown to put together a complaint, so these guys can be taken off the street. I'll have to brief my boss, and get him ready for a press conference. I'll get you a copy of the complaint so your Assistant Director can coordinate with us. Good job. And tell Michaels he pulled this one out of his ass, and had me sweating for a while."

"Check and see what they have on the liberal channels. Bet they are blaming the Tea Party." said Kirkland. Whitaker hit the remote a few times, but the screen went blank. "What the hell's the matter with the TV?"

Kirkland was unconcerned. "They probably shut down a lot of the communication systems for fear of the possibility that an additional strike will happen. Call a taxi or a car service if you can find one out here in the sticks, and I will cancel the helicopter, which most likely won't run anyway once the news gets around. We can walk down to the country club, and have it pick us up there. Make sure they take credit cards."

Kirkland sat back in the leather chair while Whitaker switched the TV channel back to Fox. Geoff Young was repeating the breaking news for the benefit of new listeners when suddenly the screen went blank. Whitaker cursed, put down the remote. He grabbed his cell phone to call for a limo service.

A half hour later, they sat quietly as the limo made its way down the service road to the Interstate, passing a Marriott Residence Inn along the way.

Inside the motel, four FBI agents from the Special Operations Tech Unit, dressed in dirty black military fatigues sat in one room, exhausted from a night of work. A couple of black backpacks lay on the floor. Their unmarked van containing a myriad of digital communication equipment, spools of wire, and attendant tools was parked in the lot outside the room. They had just finished watching a small television monitor amongst other technical equipment with cable running out the rear window, and into the adjoining woods. They were in a good mood and making small talk.

Eddie Michaels appeared from the adjoining room. "You guys did a tremendous job, and I owe you," he said to the group. "I'd buy you a few beers, but it's too early."

"I'll take a rain check," one of the agents said, "next time I see you at the local watering hole across from the office."

"I'll second that." said another.

They had just finished watching the performance of Geoff Young, the Fox News reporter who was a good friend of the New York FBI as a result of getting the timely scoop on many important stories. He frequently was leaked information when it suited the Bureau's purposes, and today was payback to which he readily obliged.

"How'd I do?" he asked as he emerged from the adjoining room while an agent packed up the backdrop that he used for his bogus broadcast.

"Just like you do every night," said Michaels. "We got what we needed, and you will get the scoop on whatever comes out of this case. Wait until you hear from me because they're some loose ends that have to be tied up. I just learned that we have two cars on their way up here to make the arrests. A warrant was just signed based on what came out on our wire. Thanks. We have our chopper on the way to pick you up at a small nearby local airport that will take you to the East 34th St. heliport."

From midnight on, the tech agents located the cable going into Kirkland's cabin. They spliced into it giving them the ability to cancel the regular programming, and broadcast the fake breaking news segment by Geoff Young live from the hotel. They had met their objective by getting Kirkland and Whitaker to discuss the conspiracy they were engaged in.

CHAPTER 34

Ride to New York City

A short time after the limo left for Westchester, Kirkland was curious that there was silence. The driver received no phone calls to caution him about traveling into the city if he had to go there.

"Driver, please put on the radio, and see if we can catch the news and weather." said Kirkland as the scenery passed by. Kirkland was facing out the rear side window, but he was seeing nothing. His mind was racing through a series of thoughts that arose, none of which was pleasant. Five minutes into the news, he knew something was wrong, and suspected that he had been had. He turned towards Whitaker, who was now visibly nervous.

"Edmund, I think we are fucked." Kirkland said stoically. "Right now, I am trying to remember what we said when the broadcast came on. There will come a time when I, and some of my best legal team can parse through a transcript, if there is one.   And right now, it adds up that there was a microphone in the cabin taking in all that we said. That whole broadcast was a sham. Somewhere along the line we made a mistake. I'm trying to figure out how and who was responsible. Probably Michael did something foolish. Much as I liked that kid, I should have gone with your plan to take him out of the picture, but if that failed, he would have all the cards, and who knows what would have happened. No matter what, I am finished as a judge. Fortunately, I do not have a wife to be concerned about. When the ex hears about this, she will probably be delighted."

"What about me?" interjected Whitaker, "My business is over. My house near the country club will be gone, my daughter will be disgraced, and my wife will most likely dump me. I'm sure the feds are looking for us right now. There is only one out."

Whitaker dialed his home on his cell phone. He didn't respond to his wife's greeting, and brusquely said "Jeannie, call Debbie at college, and tell her we have to leave town. Money will continue to be put in her checking account, and she should not worry. We will be in touch. Meanwhile, pack a light suitcase, get our passports and the ten grand cash I have in the linen closet. Go to the Rye Hilton and wait for me." A series of "buts" came from the other end of the line. Whitaker paid no attention, and ended with "Just do what I say. And bring the package on the top shelf of the linen closet." She knew he was referring to his .38 caliber Chief Special revolver.

He turned towards Kirkland, who was still looking out the window, silent in thought.

"I'm going to go to that little island home I have off of the coast of Greece. I have money in a bank there that should last for a while. I'll figure something out from there. I don't believe the Greeks will extradite me."

Whitaker told the driver to go to the Rye Hilton rather than his home while Kirkland contemplated his next move.

"Driver, rather than the 87th Street address, take me to the Union League Club, 38 East 37th Street," Kirkland ordered.

He turned towards Whitaker. "I can stay there for a while, contact my lawyer to figure out the best way to play this. I don't know if you should leave the country. A sure sign of guilt. Better you stay here, and hide out until I can find out what the charges are, if any, and then we fight it. The question is did they turn Michael. If that is the case, we're done."

"Judge, there is too much at stake. Besides going to jail, I can lose everything with the new forfeiture provisions. I've got to take a shot, and hope Customs doesn't have a lookout for me. The quicker I get out of here, the better. How do I reach you?"

Kirkland thought for a moment. "Call the Union League Club, and ask for a Mr. Kaye. I will alert the desk to find me. Don't use your cell phone. Use a pay phone if you can find one these days, or get a burner phone. When you get overseas, pick up an international one, and call me so I have your contact information."

CHAPTER 35

Freedom Tower

Earlier at midnight, Willie O'Shea was frustrated as he led the two FBI agents around the 59th floor of the Freedom Tower. He had a bolt cutter, and had already had cut into a few construction shanties, those where the agents had a hard time picking the locks. Several locked cages containing acetylene tanks were opened, but after a quick test, that's all they were.

Below, a block away, the evidence technicians from the laboratory just arrived, and waited in a large step van. Their orders were to wait for a call when something was found.

"Listen lads, we've checked all the logical places where some tanks could be hidden. From what I heard, there are more than five or six, and probably are stashed in one place. You tell me now, what's the importance of acetylene tanks. They can't blow up."

The agents were briefed about the sarin gas,

but did not want to tell O'Shea for fear that he would leave the area after telling everyone at the site to get out as well.

"Willie, we're not certain. Could be a harmless bomb threat or could be something more serious."

"I told Eddie that this guy Burke was a little weird, and he should keep an eye on him. Don't know what you dug up about his background. There must be something because I doubt that he brought the tanks into the site as a favor for someone, but it is a possibility. There are about 20 trades here that have occasion to use acetylene, and are spread out so much they could possibly use several tanks rather than moving them up and down the floors. It would take a while to check with all the foreman. We'd have to wait until tomorrow."

"We don't have that luxury, we have to find them soon," one of the agents said with a sense of urgency as they walked the perimeter of the 60th floor."

"Well, well," said O'Shea. Look what we got here," as he stopped by an inner wall a few feet from the elevator shaft.

"What are you talking about Willie?"

"This gang box here. Every trades got a few that they keep valuable tools in so they won't walk away. Get what I mean?"

"So?" was the response from one of the agents.

O'Shea pointed to the one in front of them. "See this box. What makes it different from the others that we passed is that it has no company name on it. No one leaves a gang box out without the company name plastered all over it."

O'Shea bent over to examine the seven by three-by-three-foot heavy metal box locked with a chain going through a hole in the top, out the side, and then joined by a solid steel padlock. He bent further to the level of the top of the box, and rubbed his hand slowly across it. O'Shea straightened up with a smile.

"Me money is on this one, boys. It's a box from WJF Plumbing. If you look closely, and smooth your hand over the top, you can see the name raised where it was painted before. Also, the lock is brand new, which you don't see around here."

"Very good Willie," said one of the agents as he knelt down, removed his lock picks from his little black bag, and went to work. In five minutes, the lock popped open.

"Bingo," the agent said as he removed the chain, and slowly raised the lid."

"Holy shit," said the other as the three men gazed at eight tanks stored in the box."

Within a half hour, O'Shea and the agents rolled the gang box onto a hoist, which took them to ground level, and out the gate to the awaiting van. The eight tanks were unloaded into the van that had a myriad of testing kits, tools, and detection devices.

"We'll call you in about an hour. That should be enough time for us to neutralize these tanks," one of the technicians said as he started to roll down the rear entrance of the van. They already had been briefed about the existence of dynamite, but were not prepared to deal with what they were about to discover.

CHAPTER 36

FBI Office

En route to the FBI Office, Gerosa dropped Larkin off in the Bronx, gave her ten $20 bills, and told her to take a taxi to his apartment, and wait for further instructions.

Two agents met the undercover car as it stopped at the bottom of the entrance ramp at 26 Federal Plaza, and took the prisoner for processing while Gerosa hurried to Dean's office for a meeting.

"Glad to see you are here in one piece. You think this guy will give up Zorn?" Dean asked as he peered over his reading glasses.

"I don't know. There was no new identity for Larkin. No money and no plane tickets. So, it's definite that they planned to kill her. Right now, the story for the locals is that I was there to do an undercover buy of some heroin, and the agent in the limo and Larkin were my backup when this guy, who was planning a rip-off of the buy money, sprang into action. We overpowered him. Brought him back here to question him, but we might have to turn him over to the Armonk PD if he doesn't talk, and we want to keep this quiet."

Michaels interrupted Gerosa as he came through the door.

"Decided to take the chopper back here with Young. Didn't want to miss the meeting." He took his seat next to Gerosa in front of Dean's desk.

'We just started, Eddie. Let me bring you up to date" Dean said. "The lab guys got a surprise when they opened up the tanks. Inside each was a cylinder of sarin gas. They knew by the markings, and didn't go any further. Also, the tanks were packed with C-4 and a blasting cap rigged with some kind of altimeter that would cause it to go off at different levels in the elevator shaft. If that happened, several floors would be filled with sarin, the most going to the lobby, and then outside where the people are coming and going through the PATH station. Would have been complete chaos.

"As you know, we got what we wanted on the mike in the cabin. The downside is that by the time we got the okay for the arrests, Kirkland and Whitaker were gone. No chopper came, so I guess they either had a car or took a car service." Michaels reported.

"What are we doing to get them?" Dean asked.

"Agents are on their way to their homes. Whitaker's is up in Rye, and Kirkland has an apartment in the city. What went on here?"

Michaels leaned back in his seat.

"As soon as I found out about the sarin, I called Mike Kossler over at the CIA, and told him about our find. If you recall a few weeks ago, the mention of sarin was brought up at one of the Homeland Security briefings. Well, Kossler came alive when I said sarin, and he will be here shortly. He requested that we hold off anything until we can work something out. Evidently, the Agency can be very embarrassed should this come out. They would have to answer plenty of questions before several committees in Washington."

"What happened at the site?" asked Michaels.

"The only people who know about the sarin are the lab guys, the three of us here and Assistant Director Malone. There is an emergency meeting going on now in Washington with the Directors of the FBI and CIA. We have all been sworn to secrecy."

"What about the arrest warrants when Kirkland and Whitaker are brought in? What happens then?" Gerosa interjected.

"I know you are not going to like this," Dean said. "But I have been talking with Siano, and nothing specific is spelled out in the complaint. You know it can be dismissed easily. The recorded conversations can be buried in our files, and we can only hope that Judge Brennan, who signed the order will do the same."

"Shit," Michaels said. "What happened with Burke at the site?"

"Your guy Willie did a great job. Obviously, he doesn't know about the sarin, but knows something was in the tanks. The lab guys got back to the site a couple of hours after they left, and met Willie around the corner, where they loaded the same gang box with the empty cylinders. Willie got the box back to its position before Burke came in. He outfitted our guys as two new workers, and they kept an eye on Burke on the 60th floor. At about 9:20 he received a phone call, and he sprang into action. He rolled the gang box to the elevator shaft, and started dumping the empty tanks down the shaft in numerical order, the way he was instructed." Dean leaned back with a slight smile. "What happened next couldn't have been better scripted."

Gerosa and Michaels were not privy to what had happened, and knew Dean was leading them on. "So?" said Michaels.

"After the empty tanks clanged to the bottom and bounced around, one of our guys called the Port Authority Police while the other went to grab Burke. At first, he was stunned by no explosion, and then ran to the outer perimeter screaming that he was fucked, and wanted to know where the helicopter was." Dean chuckled and continued.

"The cops arrive with Willie who tells them that the guy has shown signs of being a little nutty, and that he tossed some empty acetylene tanks that he had stolen from the other trades, apparently hid them, and today threw them down the elevator shaft."

"God damn" Gerosa said. "You can't make this shit up."

"That's not all," said Dean. "The cops arrive, and Burke starts screaming that he is working for the CIA, and that a helicopter is supposed to come by and pick him up. He continues his screaming as they take him away. Willie gave a statement to the cops that they were getting ready to fire Burke because he was becoming delusional.

"I checked with Port Authority PD, and they said there was no apparent danger to the site, and that a Kieran Burke was taken to Bellevue psych ward where he is in a padded cell. Obviously, they don't want anything to come out that anyone working on behalf of a terrorist organization made it onto the site. So that's where we stand."

Susan brought in a tray of coffee, and left it on the coffee table. As the three of them moved to the couch, Gerosa winked at Susan. She responded by mouthing, "Call me."

Shortly after discussing loose ends that had to be tied up, Susan came in, and announced that Kossler was outside.

"Show him in," said Dean.

Kossler fit the Agency's bureaucratic Washington DC mold. Dressed in a dark gray suit and muted tie, Kossler was a former one star in the Defense Intelligence Agency. He normally would exude confidence, which was his trademark at meetings with the president or testifying before a congressional committee, but today was different.

"Rick, I want to thank you for calling me first, and not letting this thing get out of our control. I don't need my face all over the networks trying to explain sarin gas. Probably shouldn't have had our rep mention it at the security meeting, but we were hoping there would be a quick resolve to the missing sarin. That didn't happen."

Kossler continued and gave the full story about the sarin, omitting only the fact that it was being bought from Iran. He didn't say where it came from, and the question was never asked, respecting his confidentiality.

"Tell us about Michael Zorn?" Dean asked.

"He was with us for a few years, and did a good job, but then left. Don't know what he was doing, but I do know that he didn't need money. Evidently had a lot from an inheritance. Has a house and wife in Scarsdale. No kids. He reappeared last year when he took the job of the New York State Homeland Security rep. I am totally against these guys, and have made my feelings known, but with Zorn I figured that he was an Agency guy, so there would be no harm. They have access to most anything they want, and get to sit in on our weekly briefings."

"Does the name Annie Larkin ring a bell?" asked Dean.

Kossler thought for a moment. "Vaguely. I recall a while back, Zorn said he was doing something off the record with her. Something about providing info re gunrunning and the new IRA. Never had anything substantive, so we basically ignored what he was doing and never reopened her as an asset. As I recall, she did something in the past for the Garda in Ireland, and was worked briefly here, but really had nothing for us."

Dean resisted asking Kossler why they didn't tell the FBI because it was a domestic matter. It would have put a damper on the meeting, and he needed everyone on the same page, primarily to cover their asses. He went on to tell Kossler what had happened at the site with Burke, and the warrant for Kirkland and Whitaker.

"Jesus Christ." Kossler said. "Why didn't you call me from the beginning? We could have worked something out together."

"Mike, it was too hush-hush. There was a federal judge possibly involved, a prominent businessman, and a possible terrorist plot to put a dent in the construction of the Freedom Tower. I apologize if you are offended." Dean knew it was easier to apologize rather than argue about the merits of cooperation with the CIA.

"Where do we go from here?" Kossler asked.

"We've got a cone of silence about this around here. Need-to-know basis. Our directors can talk about this, and discuss strategically how to handle any inquiries at their level, but the shots are being called from here. We have warrants for Kirkland and Whitaker, and are trying to locate Zorn. We don't have enough for a warrant for him. Want to put him under surveillance for now."

"Rick, please keep me advised, and if there is anything you need from the Agency, let me know."

After several minutes of small talk, Kossler left while Dean, Michaels and Gerosa reviewed what had transpired, and waited for a call from the agents on the street to update them.

"I almost forgot Eddie, your buddy Geoff did a good job getting what we wanted off Kirkland and Whitaker" Dean said. "What does he want in return, the usual?"

"You got it," answered Michaels. "A scoop on the story, and probably again when the next big case comes down."

Dean thought for a moment. "Unfortunately, there might not be any story for publication here. Not for the press, and not for your memoirs."

CHAPTER 37

EPILOGUE

Edmund Whitaker

The car service dropped off Whitaker in the driveway of the Rye Hilton, where his Cadillac Escalade was parked in the lot. His wife was waiting in one of the luxury suites.

Sitting on one of the lounge chairs as he came through the door, the attractive, well-kept middle-aged blonde housewife didn't look like her usual self. No time to discuss what the emergency was, she obeyed her husband and did as she was told. Her time was limited to blue jeans, tennis shoes and an old white turtleneck cashmere sweater. Her hair in a ponytail, she had no time for brushing and makeup.

"Okay Ed, what's going on?" Jeanne Whitaker was used to impromptu moves on her husband's part, but few that included her. And there was the call to their daughter. "Why are we here, and where are we going?" She could see her husband was troubled, but didn't press the issue.

"I need to get away for a while, and called the pilots to prepare the company jet to take us to the small Mykonos Island airport. It's international, and from there we can go to our home on Anafi."

Jeannie thought that unusual because she had never been there. She knew he went there on occasion for high-level business meetings, but that was all.

She knew her husband well. "Stop the bullshit, Ed. What kind of trouble are you in?" She picked up the small box containing his pistol. "And what the hell is this for?"

"Honey, trust me. I think I'm in a little bit of trouble, and I need to get away. It will probably all blow over. We'll be back in a month."

Whitaker turned on the television to the news channel to see if there was anything about the Freedom Tower. More importantly, anything about him or Kirkland having arrest warrants out for them. He glanced at his watch. It was a little after noon.

"The plane won't be ready until around 6 this evening, so let's get some rest." He went to the service bar, and pulled out two small bottles of bourbon.

The Escalade sped across Interstate 287, and went north on I 684 to the turnoff to the Westchester County Airport. Whitaker parked in the General Aviation parking lot. Inside the office, he met the pilots who had already taken care of the necessary paperwork and the fueling. The flight to Mykonos Island took off an hour before the Westchester County Police were notified that the feds were interested in Whitaker, and should delay him if he or Kirkland intended to go anywhere in a helicopter or winged aircraft. They were unaware that Whitaker had a leased late model Challenger 605 that had trans-Atlantic capability. The lease was in one of the spin-off companies of Coordinated Technologies.

The thirteen-hour flight was uneventful for Whitaker and his wife, who slept part of the way. The small airport had a one-man customs booth, and the agent recognized Whitaker as a resident and waved him through with a "Welcome back" greeting. From there they took a small seaplane to the dock outside his waterfront home on Anfi. The home was well kept by a regular house watch contractor who kept it clean and functional.

For the first week, Whitaker religiously checked the American news that he had beamed in via satellite, but found nothing about an incident at the site or anything about the arrest or indictment of federal judge Kirkland. He had everything in place at his business, his next in command running it, and keeping in constant communication with him. He expected that agents would show up with a subpoena for him or the business would be hit with a search warrant. But nothing. Not even a telephone call from the FBI. His wife turned towards him as they sat on the porch overlooking where the Aegean Sea blends into the Mediterranean.

"So, are we here for good? No more parties at the country club. No more golf for you. Are we officially retired?" she said sarcastically.

"No. We can take regular trips to the mainland. Or travel Europe for a while. There is plenty of money that I put in the banks here, and Debbie can come here for her vacations from college. In a couple of months, we can go back home. Everything will be the same." He lied, and was confused as to why no one was looking for him.

The following week, Whitaker began experiencing abdominal pain with frequent nausea. He treated himself with a variety of over-the-counter medicines that proved ineffective. He eventually went to Athens where he saw a battery of specialists. The final diagnosis was advanced pancreatic cancer, and he was dead in a month.

CHAPTER 38

Eddie Michaels

The FBI had been monitoring Whitaker's activity since he arrived through a personal contact with the Greek National Police and Interpol. Dean was at his desk when the call came in from Captain Nikos Plagos advising him that Whitaker passed away in an Athens Hospital. He immediately called Michaels.

"Eddie, it has finally happened. Whitaker is dead. As far as I know, he left no memoirs. Don't know what we would have done should he have come back here, but this resolves that issue. Did you make the right decision?"

"I'll know in a few months. After the excitement of the retirement racket and the quick wedding, Nancy and I are finally getting to know each other. When are you coming down? The condo here in Naples is nice, and only a couple of hours away from Dick in Pompano. If it was closer, I could get into trouble with him, and his nightlife chasing women."

"Stay in touch and keep a room open for me."
Rick said as he hung up the phone.

CHAPTER 39

Judge Robert Kirkland

Judge Terrence Brennan was a friend of the FBI, but now was in his chambers glowering at Supervisor Rick Dean and AUSA Siano.

"Okay gentlemen. Can you tell why the hell you want all the court orders for your expedite terrorism wiretap sealed by me along with the results? I heard the tapes, but didn't see the transcripts because there weren't any. At least that is what you told me, Rick." He shifted his gaze directly at Dean, who was silent.

Siano spoke first. "Your honor, I would never ask you to do anything that was not legal, and know you would never do so anyway. Probably have me disbarred, but there are extenuating circumstances here relating to terrorism." Siano continued quoting a statute giving Brennan the latitude to do as he asked. Dean then gave Brennan the full story of CIA, FBI, and the attempted terrorist act at the Freedom Tower, and sat like a schoolboy ready to be scolded by the principal.

"The problem here is Judge Kirkland. We are friends by virtue of our positions. If all this disappears, what is he going to do? He knows the full story, and his role in it. Will he be silent, and let it go away, or is he going to press the issue and attempt to clear himself of any wrongdoing? And blast the FBI, and possibly get you both indicted for something or at least fired. Do you know where the judge is now?"

"We killed the warrant for him, as you know." Siano answered.

"Well, where is he? He missed his court date yesterday, but that was only one day since the incident at the Freedom Tower."

"Don't know," said Dean sheepishly. "We tried his apartment. Thought he might have shown up here for a court date, but nothing."

"Let's see what happens with him. We can decide then whether both you guys go to jail." The judge smiled, knowing that he would do all he could to protect the two excellent government employees in front of him.

The maid at the Union League knocked on the door of room 431 after working her way up the hallway, cleaning rooms, and replacing toiletries, sheets and towels from the cart alongside her. Presuming that the occupant was gone after the third knock, she used her master key to enter. The bed didn't appear slept in, just messed up a little. A partially filled glass of scotch whiskey sat on the nightstand. She quickly straightened the bed, noting that the sheets were neither wrinkled too much nor stained, and could be used for the next guest.

An easy room by some standards, she thought, recalling the effort it took to clean up after a party was had with three or four wealthy businessmen. Hoping the bathroom would be similar, and she could take it easy, she entered to replace the towels and do her cleaning.

"O my God," she muttered as she raced to the house phone, and hysterically called the desk for help.

In the empty tub lay Judge Robert Kirkland, his eyes closed, the blood from his slit wrists coagulating at the bottom, and soaking through his undershorts and shirt. A half full bottle of Macallan 12-year-old scotch sat beside the tub.

CHAPTER 40

Michael Zorn

"Do it now" was the command Michael Zorn gave on his cell phone. It was 9:20 on September 12.

Kieran Burke asked one question. "Is the chopper on the way?"

"It is on the way." Zorn said with assurance.

After ending the brief call, Burke moved towards the gang box, and proceeded with his plan.

Zorn was calling from JFK International Airport in the Lufthansa terminal. He was booked on the 10:35 flight to Frankfurt, Germany under an assumed identity. He was now watching the CNN news in the waiting area. For the past several years after his employment with the Agency, he managed to siphon off thousands of dollars, and deposit them in a Swiss bank account. With the proper forged documents, he was able to liquidate the trust fund left for him by his father, and sent that also to a Swiss bank account.

At 9:30, when CNN failed to report any new news, Zorn dialed the number of his operative that was to take out Annie Larkin. His phone rang unattended as it lay on the desk of the agent who was assigned to investigate the operative's background, and get statements from Gerosa and the undercover limo driver. He took a chance, and answered it.

"Hello."

Zorn silently cursed as he hung up the phone. He went to the gate to await boarding under the name of Michael Miller, an employee of a fictitious hedge fund.

A day after the event at the Freedom Tower, Dean met with Kossler at the local CIA office at Kossler's request.

"Rick, have you located Zorn yet?" Kossler asked.

"No. There was an attempt on Annie Larkin's and our undercover's life during a supposed meeting in Armonk. We believe Larkin was being set up, so our undercovers were there to protect her. We ended up arresting Walter McGeehan, a former Navy SEAL and black ops operative who was given a dishonorable discharge after a series of events in Iraq, the details of which are not necessary. McGeehan flipped after eight hours of questioning, and being faced with a long prison term. He is part of a renegade private security firm that will do anything for money. We are looking into them as I speak."

"I guess the answer to my question is that Zorn is gone."

"We only have an assaulting a federal officer charge against him. If we get him, I'm not sure what he would do. He can't give us Judge Kirkland, who was found dead this morning at the Union League Club, an apparent suicide. He can't give us Whitaker, who we now have located on an island off the coast of Greece. He is being monitored by the police over there in case we want to do something with him, but right now, the arrest warrant and our wiretap have all been killed by the judge at our request with the blessing of both our directors. If all this came out, everyone would be embarrassed. People would believe that the Freedom Tower, or T1 as they call it today, would lose tenants, and visitors would not go there fearing that if it could be penetrated during construction, it could be penetrated almost anytime. All the publicity about the security at the site would mean nothing."

Kossler leaned back in his chair. "Rick, I have to tell you something that has to stay between us. Our Office of Professional Responsibility has been looking at Zorn for a while. Some of his expenses are being questioned, and in some cases it appears that they can't be justified."

"Can you be more specific?"

"When he was with the Agency, he was

in our Berlin Station, and assigned to develop intelligence on the Russians. A large amount of money was spent on one Yuri Osterman, a KGB agent assigned to the Russian embassy in Berlin, ostensibly as a cultural liaison for the performing arts. He gave little information, but we believe he was trying to turn Zorn, and it appears much of the info that Zorn reported was bullshit and public information. We could never prove anything, and our investigation died. The only good that came out of it is that after Zorn left, his replacement turned Osterman, and he came to our side, and has been valuable."

"Zorn could have gone back to Berlin," Dean said, "where he knows his way around, obviously in a new identity. We spoke to his wife, and she couldn't care less. They were on the verge of a divorce, have no kids, and she has a pretty good job as an exec with a bank. We'll let you know if we find him. Interpol has his picture and all relevant information."

After a few days in Frankfurt, Michael Zorn decided to go to Berlin, and follow up on a plan he concocted while traveling. He could always use extra cash.

"Please give a message to Mr. Osterman that Michael would like some tickets to tonight's opera." Zorn spoke to the receptionist in English, and she advised him that Osterman would receive the message. This was Zorn's previous means to communicate with Osterman. It was a signal for him to meet Zorn in the men's room of a local museum at precisely 7:00 pm.

Zorn came out of one of the stalls. Osterman was punctual, washing his hands as Zorn used the basin next to him.

"It's been a while," said Osterman in fluent English. "I presume you are well, and back with the Agency."

"Not quite. I'm here to make a deal. I give you a list of known CIA operatives in Germany and surrounding areas, and you give me one million dollars. Also, a guarantee of asylum if things get too hot for me here. We will meet here in two days, and you can tell me the arrangements where we can make the trade. Understand?"

Osterman thought for a moment. "I think that might work. I will see you here in two days with the details. Goodnight Mr. Zorn."

Zorn was relaxed as the taxi made its way to the Museum Berggruen in Berlin, where he leaped up the steps to the entrance in anticipation. Barely anyone was there at this time, and he walked around pretending to study the various paintings as he repeatedly glanced at his watch, waiting for the appointed hour. At exactly 7:00 pm, he entered the washroom and smiled as no one else was visible. As he approached a bathroom sink, he heard the door to one of the stalls open. Believing it was Osterman, he slowly turned.

Michael Zorn never heard the series of the pops from the silencer, and was dead before he hit the floor. The man in a raincoat pocketed his pistol and left.

CHAPTER 41

Willie O'Shea

Willie O'Shea looked at the caller ID on his cell phone and grinned.

"Eddie, how're you doin'?"

"Very good, Willie. Sorry that I haven't called earlier, but I retired, got married, and bought a condo all in the same month. How about you?"

"I had thirty-eight years with the union, and with all the money I made down there with the overtime, I had to retire or lose money. Just got back from a trip to Ireland, and am thinking about getting a place in Sarasota."

"Come on down," Michaels said. "The weather's great. I'm not that far away."

"This may shock you," O'Shea said. "I have given up the butts, cut out anything with sugar in it, and am walking every day. Doctor's orders of course. I'd never do it on my own. Also, takin' up golf."

"Listen Willie. Has anyone from any newspaper, government agency, or anybody contacted you about that night at the site, and what went on?" Michaels was serious for a moment.

"Nothin' Eddie."

"Good because no one would believe you anyway. They'd put you in a rubber room like Burke."

"Is he still there?"

"Yeah, and he will be there for a long time. He keeps ranting that he works for the CIA, the IRA, the government and whoever he can think up. Also, he attacked a couple of guards. "

"Good. Never liked him."

"Well, Willie, you started this whole thing going. I can't give you any details so you can just speculate went on in addition to your end. I can't even get you any award, but within a few days, the case of Jameson I promised you will arrive minus one bottle for me."

CHAPTER 42

Annie Larkin

Annie Larkin stayed at Gerosa's apartment for three days after the incident at the motel. After lengthy interviews by Bureau agents, Gerosa got her off from being prosecuted because of her cooperation. He also had her submit to a polygraph exam that showed that she genuinely believed that she was working for the CIA. As a bonus, Gerosa arranged for her to get a new identity through the witness protection program, but she refused to be relocated. A moderate sum of money would be wired to a Western Union Station in whatever city she happened to be in at the time. She was last heard from in Gulf Shores, Alabama where she was renting a waterfront apartment.

When the dust settled, all the paperwork involving the investigation was put in a box and driven to FBI Headquarters where it would be stored in a special archive section.

Three days later, in the early evening, Dick Gerosa sat on a barstool in Stark's restaurant across the street from Federal Plaza, slowly sipping on a Stella. He had cleaned out his apartment, and would be spending the night at a Marriott near La Guardia Airport. Tomorrow he would board a flight to Fort Lauderdale, where he would take a taxi home.

"Is this the last hurrah?" asked Rick Dean as he and Eddie Michaels pulled up stools next to his.

"Probably," answered Gerosa, "but then again, you never know. Life is good in Florida, but it can get boring. As you know, I like the thrill of the chase every so often."

He gave a wolfish grin.

"Chasing criminals or woman?" asked Michaels.

"Both," was the response.

They were enjoying the second round of their favorite beverage when Gerosa felt a tap on his shoulder. Sue Wollman was standing behind him gazing at her watch.

"So? I'm on time. When are we leaving?" She was grinning at her boss, Dean, who knew she had a date with Gerosa that evening.

"Let me finish my beer, and say goodbye to my two amigos. Meanwhile, pull up a stool. What are you drinking?"

Gerosa turned towards his two friends. "I'm taking her to a nice Italian restaurant out by La Guardia."

Gerosa again adapted easily to his life of leisure in Pompano. He had fleeting thoughts about writing a book about some of his exploits while in the Bureau. A novel based on facts, but totally fiction. He had finished a day at the beach, and a happy hour at the tiki bar, and was catching the evening news, deciding whether to eat in or go out. He was on his lanai looking at the Atlantic from his 10th floor condo and lamented that his former girlfriends abandoned him for new relationships. Not only that, he recalled the words of Susan Wollman, "Absence does not make the heart grow fonder," when he came back to New York. "I guess she was right" he said to himself.

A knock on the door interrupted his thoughts. "Well, I'll be damned," he said as he looked at the blond, neatly dressed in Florida garb, carrying two suitcases.

"I was taking a chance coming here, and hope you didn't have a steady companion. Do you?"

"Come on in," Gerosa said as he eyed her from head to toe. "You are welcome to stay here as long as you want. I was thinking of you." He lied.

"Good to see you. The only change is that my hair is now blonde," said Annie Larkin as she moved towards the bedroom with her suitcases.

Printed in Great Britain
by Amazon

37221420R00169